Jane Jobson Scott

The Skeleton in the Cupboard

Volume 1

Jane Jobson Scott

The Skeleton in the Cupboard
Volume 1

ISBN/EAN: 9783337423247

Printed in Europe, USA, Canada, Australia, Japan

Cover: Foto ©Andreas Hilbeck / pixelio.de

More available books at **www.hansebooks.com**

The

Skeleton in the Cupboard.

IN TWO VOLUMES.

VOL. I.

By LADY SCOTT,

Authoress of 'The Henpecked Husband,' 'The Only Child,' &c.

London:

Saunders, Otley, and Co., Conduit Street.

1860.

The Skeleton
in the Cupboard.

CHAPTER I.

In the prettiest of the London suburbs, on the brink of a wide common, and standing within its own iron gates, there gleamed through its nest of trees one of the most imposing and complete of what house agents would designate "modern mansions," simply called, by its contented owners, The Laurels.

There are some houses that bear about them the stamp of wealth. From the moment that the iron gates open to receive you on the delicate gravel, to that in which you find yourself passing through the richly carpeted hall into the still more costly drawing-room, you feel that you are breathing the mysterious atmosphere of money! money! money!

And now that house bore an aspect of more than usual beauty and comfort. There was going to be a wedding there, the wedding of the only daughter, the only child and heiress, and Mr. and Mrs. Blackstone were sparing neither pains, nor time, nor trouble, nor money, to celebrate the event with all the honour due to the brilliant alliance which Euphemia, their fondly-loved Phemy, was about to contract.

To the astonishment—almost to the consternation—of the parents who lived only for her, and who, because she had attained the age of twenty-two, they had imagined they should keep with them for ever, this young girl had, at last, made her selection, or rather, her time had come, and she was now on the eve of her grand match.

Destiny, one fine day, had brought, in a curious and unexpected manner, a middle-aged baronet to The Laurels—Sir Felix Bohun of Bohun Court—and he, who had been accidentally drawn thither on a matter of business in which it was within Mr. Blackstone's vocation to assist him, at last found himself impelled by a question, not of law, but of love; and ended by laying his heart and all his wide worldly possessions at the feet of that fair creature whom he invited to become the third Lady Bohun.

Dazzled and delighted, for Euphemia was ambitious, the young girl did not keep the trembling captive long in suspense. It is true that Sir Felix had seen more than five-and-forty summers, and that in marrying him she would have to run the chance of comparison with two predecessors, both ladies of high degree; but she was not one to care for either of these little drawbacks.

" Had he been a widower with half-a-dozen grown up daughters, mamma," said she, as she watched the sealing of the letter of acceptation, " we might have some just grounds for hesitation, and, I dare say, I should have said no, immediately ; but, as it is, he is a bridegroom without encumbrances, and I like him all the better for his age. A younger man might not have given me so much my own way, and that I must have, as you well know, darling mother, even if I married the Marquis of Carabas."

Mrs. Blackstone had no arguments to urge against this; she was only so afraid that the disparity would make him an uncongenial companion to one so full of life, and spirits, and energy as Phemy ; and at this the light-hearted

girl laughed heartily. (She was incomparably
more worldly than that trembling anxious mother.)

"Don't fear, mamma," said she, "never mind
his age. It is a brilliant match, and even had he
been twenty years older, it is one which will be
envied, right and left, from one end of our circle
to the other!"

Truly spoken, fair Euphemia! you knew well
enough, when you accepted Sir Felix Bohun,
that the world would say you were marrying an
elderly widower; but as long as the Bohun
diamonds, and Bohun Court could be held up
against the malicious assertion, you might laugh
the world and its remarks to scorn.

Mr. Blackstone looked grave when called upon
to give his sanction to what he considered the
unequal match.

"I do not like the idea of Phemy's marrying
so completely out of her sphere," said he, as he
talked the subject over with his wife; but
feminine eyes seldom see an eligible alliance in
this light, and though Mrs. Blackstone had her
own private fears and misgivings, and had even
repeated the hint to Phemy that the disparity
between them was the point to which she could
not reconcile herself, she would not have a word
said about the inequality. Phemy, in the eyes

of her doating mother, was a fitting bride for
any lord in the land, and as for taking her out of
her sphere......

" When a young girl marries, my dear," was
her reply, as she bridled up with proper maternal
pride and dignity, " one would surely rather see
her rise higher in the world than sink to a lower
place......"

" I did not wish that," exclaimed Mr. Blackstone, hastily, " I meant more on her own level."

" Oh, no," said his wife, in a tone of decision ;
" Phemy is worth more than that."

So Mr. Blackstone was silenced and corrected,
and never ventured to interpose his objections
again, and the wedding preparations went on.

It still wanted three weeks to the happy day—
that day termed, by general consent, " the happy
day !"—when all the parties concerned have
arrived at the very last pitch of confusion, excitement, discomfort, and exhaustion; when your
house is turned out of windows for the guests, as
completely as is your purse for the *trousseau*, and
everybody, cold and smart, shivers smilingly
about the church and whispers to everybody else,
" What an uncomfortable thing a wedding
is ! "

But almost all the preparations were concluded,

even to the new gravelling of the approach to the house. All that money could do had been done, and Euphemia Blackstone was to be attended to church by as gay a bevy of bridesmaids as ever crowded round a more fashionable altar.

There remained but one vacuum to be filled up —the future Lady Bohun must have a maid of her own—as yet, she had shared her mother's— but now there must be " my lady's maid," and every train brought down some fresh "young person " for the situation.

Hitherto none had suited, and Mrs. Blackstone was becoming perfectly rabid. Every time the footman announced that there was another "young person," her gestures of impatience and despair increased with such violence, that, at last, the man seemed frightened to open the door. But Mrs. Blackstone was particular, and it was not every one who could please her. Some of these applicants were too smart, some too dowdy, some too stout, some too short. It must be a very nice-looking person to wait on Lady Bohun-to-be, not merely for the sake of personal satisfaction, but because Mrs. Blackstone wished her daughter to make her first appearance amongst the stately old servants at Bohun Court, of whom Sir Felix was never tired of talking, attended by some one calculated to uphold both her own dignity and that of her young mistress.

"Nothing like making a good show," was her constant maxim; "if you do not think well of yourself, nobody else will think well of you; I can trust to your supporting your dignity up-stairs, my Phemy, but it must be supported downstairs too; so a meek, mild, milk-and-water maid will never do for Lady Bohun......"

"Say, rather, for the late Miss Blackstone," laughed the gay bride; "for the truth is, mamma, you are a little bit afraid people may think me not quite worthy to step into the shoes of the two former high-born dames of Bohun Court, but never fear! I shall not want that kind of support, I know pretty well how to stand up for myself—at the same time I wish we *could* find a nice person, if only that I might get accustomed to her before I leave home."

Not many minutes after this wish had been breathed, the footman's head was partly seen at the half opened door; he had long ceased to open it boldly and show himself.

"If you please, ma'am, a young person for the lady's maid's place;" and for the hundred and fiftieth time she was desired to walk in.

Tall and slender, very calm of countenance, and

staid in demeanour, a person of an indefinite age
stood immediately before the mother and daughter,
and at one glance the quick eye of Mrs. Blackstone had taken a general and satisfactory survey
of her.

"This is the best we have seen," flashed through
her mind, and then the usual inquiries began.

"You are accustomed to all the duties of a lady's
maid?"

"Perfectly, ma'am."

"And your last situation?"

"Lady Mary Topham; I lived with her ladyship six years......"

"And your reason for leaving?"

"Her ladyship died, ma'am; but these testi-
monials which I have received from the whole
family, as well as the legacy that Lady Mary left
me, will speak sufficiently, I hope, as to the confidential position I occupied."

Mrs. Blackstone gave a little cough.

"Ah! yes; but my daughter requires merely a
lady's maid. You understand?"

"Perfectly, ma'am. It was Lady Mary's pleasure to place confidence in me. I never sought
it......"

"Hem—yes—you seem young, rather......"

"I am forty, ma'am."

" Forty? good gracious ! you look about five-
and-twenty. Are you sure? but of course ! goodness me—forty ! Euphemia, my dear."

The young lady was pretending to write a letter,
and only just glanced once upwards. " I do not
think age signifies, mamma," she said.

" Well, then," pursued Mrs. Blackstone, on
whom the manners, appearance, and language of
the person before her were gradually making their
due impression, " about hair-dressing and dress-
making, and all that ?"

" Hair-dressing, dress-making, and millinery of
every description," was the reply; " but Lady
Mary never had her dresses made at home."

" Nor should I, of course," interposed the bride
elect, hastily.

" But, my dear, it is necessary that your maid
should possess these acquirements, even if you
should not require to call them into use," said
Mrs. Blackstone, with a sort of calm severity, and
then she went on. " To whom can I apply for
your character, supposing we engage you ?"

" To the Countess of Merivale, ma'am, Lady
Mary's mamma, with whom I lived eleven years."

" What! before you went to Lady Mary ?"

" I was the Countess's own maid, ma'am ; but
when Lady Mary married Mr. Topham, her

mamma wished **** to have a confidential person
about her. I mean that her ladyship was very
young, and, in short, it was always understood
that......"

"Dear me," ejaculated Mrs. Blackstone again,
"now that is quite a curious coincidence, is it not,
Phemy? perhaps," she added, turning to the lady's
maid, "you are not aware that I am requiring
you for my daughter under very similar circumstances—in fact, on the occasion of her marriage—
to—to......" (human nature could not contain it)
—"to Sir Felix Bohun, of Bohun Court."

"I know Bohun Court, ma'am," was the quiet
reply.

Mrs. Blackstone looked puzzled. "Really!
how do you know it?"

"In the time of the first Lady Bohun, we used
to stay there, ma'am—also in the time of the
second Lady Bohun, who was a cousin of Lady
Merivale's."

Mrs. Blackstone was silent from pure astonishment. Either this was a very singular coincidence,
or else the young woman must have heard of Sir
Felix's projected marriage, and offered herself, on
the chance, to Lady Bohun the third.

Euphemia sat colouring to the tips of her fingers. She could not quite make up her mind as

to whether it would be quite pleasant to have a person about her who had actually known both the former wives. Yet how nice looking she was! so simple, so neat, so quiet, and so ladylike.

" A person I might even walk out with," she thought to herself; " yet still......"

Mrs. Blackstone was in very much the same dilemma. She wanted to ascertain her daughter's sentiments, but in the presence of the third person she felt this was impossible. She must get the young woman out of the room somehow, but not out of the house, for fear of losing her. A person with such recommendations would not be long in finding a situation ; so, as the next train to town would not start for another hour, she would offer her a cup of tea, and in the mean time confer with Euphemia and Mr. Blackstone. Unfortunately Sir Felix, who could no doubt have told them all about her, was down at Bohun Court, making the final preparations.

" Well," said she, after this mental colloquy, " I should like just to think over the subject for a little while with my daughter, and as the train does not return to town for an hour or more, it will also give us both time to remember anything we may have omitted to mention. I did not ask you your name ?"

" Mira Ponsford, ma'am."

Poor Mrs. Blackstone having already given utterance to her astonishment on two previous occasions during this interview, and been reproved for such a breach of decorum and dignity by a fire of looks from the bright eyes of her daughter, she was afraid to utter the "good gracious" which was on her lips, but she paused, nevertheless.

" Mira?" she said, interrogatively, " is that the name by which you have been in the habit of being called? because......"

A very faint smile trembled on the lips of the lady's maid.

" I have always been called Ponsford, ma'am," was her answer, and there was just sufficient intonation of reproof in her voice as she spoke, to make Miss Blackstone exclaim, " *Of course,* mamma," and carry her mother emphatically out of the room.

Before the next train started for London, Ponsford was engaged as the future Lady Bohun's maid, and on talking it over, all parties seemed pleased. Mr. Blackstone had of course a few words to say against it, but he was so much accustomed to being "put down," that he thought nothing of any objection he might advance, being immediately negatived.

He did not quite like the idea of Phemy's being attended by a person who seemed "high"—he had no pride, and though he was certainly elated at the match his daughter was so unexpectedly making, he did not hold his head a bit the higher for it, nor did he wish people to think better of him for it. Now these were sentiments which were very distasteful to both his wife and daughter. Phemy was going to move in a new sphere, and so they both thought that the people about her ought to belong to that raised sphere also.

"Ponsford looks the sort of person who would be quite a comfort to Phemy," said her mother; and Phemy added, "And save me such a world of trouble, knowing so well all about Bohun Court, and the sort of people who have been in the habit of staying there."

Mr. Blackstone said, "Humph!" but did not look convinced. He thought forty rather old too.

"Oh dear no!" cried Mrs. Blackstone, "not when the person has all the appearance of youth to add to the experience of age."

In short, it was decided that Ponsford was to be the person, and so Mr. Blackstone forbore to urge any further objections. He had only a few words to say by way of humble caution before the subject entirely dropped, and these were,

" Well, my dear, whatever you think conducive
to your comfort and happiness, shall of course be
done, only my old mother used to say, and I believe very truly, be master or mistress of your
establishment whatever be your station in life.
Be kind, but preserve your supremacy; no tyranny
like the tyranny of a servant !"

CHAPTER II.

WHAT did Mr. Blackstone, good easy man, gain by his interference in domestic matters? What does anybody ever gain for giving the advice for which they are solicited? Nothing. He had been consulted, it is true; that compliment had certainly been paid him, but his opinions had not met with that respect and obedience which one would have expected, considering that it was generally supposed Mrs. and Miss Blackstone never did anything without "consulting Mr. Blackstone."

Phemy Blackstone was young, gay, and very pretty; full of health and spirits, exuberant with happiness, words of advice and caution fell lightly on her ear, and the future was to her nothing but a still brighter phase of what had ever been to her a bright existence. All her life long, her father and mother had lived but for her, and now

another devoted heart was a toy in her hands.
All her life long she had been nursed in wealth
and luxury; now rank was to be added to these
advantages. In truth, it was enough to turn a
young girl's head; it was as if the cup were full
of prosperity to the very brim, and as for any
drawback, how could that be?

" How odd papa is !" were all the thanks the
tender, loving, anxious old man—for both he and
the mother were old for so young a daughter—
got for his pains. " How very odd he is ! What
an idea about my not being mistress of everything, and about the tyranny of a servant, too
mamma. What did he mean?"

" Oh! I know that old story so well," said Mrs.
Blackstone, smiling. " From the very day your
papa and I married, that old sentence of his has
'been ready for every occasion."

" But why, mamma? How? How can any
servant tyrannize? What does he mean?"

" My dear, there was an old story, something
that always made my blood run cold, of a clerk,
an old, old man, too, in your grandfather's count-
ing-house, who gained such an ascendancy in the
family that their very souls hardly appeared to be
their own, so fearful was his influence, and their
dread of him. At your grandfather's death-bed

the scenes were so dreadful that, your papa says, they have haunted him ever since. Had not your papa worked hard—slaved indeed—for the fortune we are blessed with, he would have been a poor man up to this day for all that his father left him! Not a farthing of your grandfather's property was secured, except a large annuity to this old man, and yet I have heard your papa say the life he led him!......ah, well!"

"But, mamma, that was a man. No woman could ever exercise tyranny?—a woman, or a maid servant rather, could never be in a position......"

"Oh! no, my dear; don't think any more of it. You have not heard the expression so often as I have, or it would not make any impression. But now, about Ponsford. We must arrange about her coming."

Yes, time was getting on. The *trousseau* was coming home day by day, and day by day, too, the excitement grew greater. Friends flocked in. The Laurels was positively besieged, and every one was charmed with the Bohun diamonds, reset, not for the third time, but for the first! The two former Ladies Bohun had been content to wear them as they were, proud of their purity, delighted when people called them *rococo*.

Not so the third Lady Bohun. "Dear Sir Felix—I like modern settings so much better—might I have just the ear-rings reset? Are you angry at my presumption? Have you any fancy for this antiquated style?"

So spake the fair *fiancée*, and what could the happy man reply, but that nothing in her could be presumption, and that he lived but to study her pleasure and happiness. The consequence was, all the diamonds were sent to Turner's, where all the Bohuns had dealt for generations, and drawings and designs were to be forwarded to Miss Blackstone.

Sir Felix was very little at The Laurels, he had so much business on his hands, but he wrote a letter to his fair Euphemia regularly every day, sometimes twice a day, and she read them the moment she had time.

One of the bridesmaid's-to-be commented one day on this stoicism, and the fair Euphemia's reply was, that she was not a literary character. She could not bear reading or writing, and reading a letter was next worst to writing one.

"But does not Sir Felix expect you to answer his epistles?"

"Oh! yes; and I do."

"What, without reading his?"

"Oh! I tell you how I manage. If I have been so busy that I have not had an instant to read his last two or three, I write him one crossed all over, and end in a clear place in a fine bold hand, 'your own loving Phemy,' and he is quite satisfied. Men never read crossed letters, so I know I am safe; and, to tell you a secret, he is what he calls rather near-sighted. I know what sort of near-sightedness it is, but never mind—dear old fellow! he sees how to choose jewels wonderfully well, and that is the sort of sight that pleases *me*, my dear!"

"Lucky Phemy!" sighed her friend; "you must give us all a helping hand when you ascend the throne. Are there no more of the same family? no brothers?"

"One brother," said Euphemia, carelessly, "only one—a younger brother, of course, but I don't know anything about him; he will not signify much to me, you know. I suppose he is in some sort of profession or other, and doubtless he will come to the wedding, but whether he is worth having or not, I cannot tell; I should say not, because a little bird whispered to me, that the Bohuns were never rich, but that both the first and second Lady Bohuns had large fortunes......"

"And the third, Phemy?"

"Ah! my dear, but the third does not mean to do what the first and second did! die first, and leave it all to Sir Felix! But, some day, I will ask all about his young brother, never fear; and if I find it worth while sending for you to Bohun Court, depend upon it I will ; and now about the bonnets......"

Miss Blackstone was a young lady gifted with a great flow of conversation, and this had hitherto been the music in which the ears of her parents chiefly delighted. To herself, also, at the present crisis, there was no theme on which she so loved to dilate, with all the powers of language, as that of her future prospects, so she talked incessantly of them, morning, noon, and night, to every friend she had, and as the prosperous of this world have many friends, the name of her listeners was Legion. It was only in strictest confidence, when their backs were fairly turned on The Laurels, that these bosom friends ventured to whisper amongst themselves, "Did you ever know any one half so absurd as Phemy Blackstone? the girl's head is turned!"

But there was one person to whom Phemy talked without the slightest misgiving as to whether her wrapt attention and sympathy were interested or not; one person who entered into all her projects, assisted her by word and by act, and with noiseless rapidity arranged the whole of the elaborate *trousseau*, and disposed it away in the various boxes without ever asking where should that go, or what should be done with this.

Many of Phemy's young friends had an eye to some of the cast-off bracelets and much of the bijouterie which the Lady Bohun-to-be now considered beneath her notice ; she was sharp enough to see all that, and a great deal more, in all those who crowded round her, save one—this one was Ponsford, the new maid, who arrived at The Laurels a week before the wedding, and who, as soon as her bonnet was off, seemed to enter upon her duties as though she had been Miss Blackstone's maid all her life.

Phemy was delighted with her, and the first day that Sir Felix arrived in town, and came out to The Laurels to dine, she began to expatiate, with her usual fluency, on the merits of Ponsford.

" And, dear Sir Felix " (she always called him "dear Sir Felix ; " he had begged her to call him Felix, but her merry young lips had never been able to achieve the feat), " dear Sir Felix, she knows all about you and Bohun Court; only think ! "

The thought brought a shadow over the brow of Sir Felix in a moment, and he paused before he answered.

" I never even heard her name," said he, at last.

" Then you are a wicked, forgetful, ungrateful man, for she holds you in the greatest respect and admiration."

" Ponsford, Ponsford?—No. I can think of no one of that name."

" Mira Ponsford; does that help you ? A tall, slight woman, very fair, very calm and concentrated (mamma calls her) in her manners; wonderful eyes, so deep, and steady, and searching ; a low, clear voice, just like a stage whisper, and without being the least handsome, a face that clings to your memory."

" Not to mine, then, fair enthusiast," said Sir Felix, smiling; "and I only hope no accomplished impostor has practised on your credulity, for I certainly have not the honour of her acquaintance."

" Now, that is very odd," persisted Euphemia ; " there must be some mistake, and the mistake, dear Sir Felix, must be yours. She was maid to a Lady Mary Topham, who was a daughter of......"

" Oh !" interrupted Sir Felix, "I used to know

all the Tophams well. Topham himself is a
hunting man in my county, and my intimate
friend. Oh, I see! Yes, yes! Of course she
has been at Bohun Court in the lifetime of Lady
Mary."

"Yes; and of Lady Merivale, her mother,"
said Euphemia.

"No doubt, no doubt—but I never saw her;
however, I dare say it is all right, and I hope she
may prove a perfect treasure for your sake; but
as to her acquaintance, that I am reluctantly
obliged to ignore, for I never even heard her
name."

"Now, that puzzles me," continued the perti-
nacious bride, who was one of those people who
will wear a subject threadbare, "because she
seems to know you so well......"

All at once a light appeared to break in upon
Sir Felix's mind, and he raised his hand with a
gesture of sudden intelligence.

"I know!" he exclaimed, "I know now!
How could I be so stupid as to forget? I perfectly remember the person you mean; not by
sight, but by reputation."

At this word Mrs. Blackstone became on the
qui vive.

"Dear me, Sir Felix—good gracious!—I hope

we have not been too precipitate? The character we received from Lady Merivale was so very satisfactory."

"Don't misunderstand me," said Sir Felix, when he could edge in a word; "I have no doubt all is right, as I before said; but what makes me remember her by reputation is, a name by which my brother always insisted on calling Lady Merivale's maid—your Ponsford, I imagine—and which used to make poor Lady Mary so angry. That name was so caught up at Bohun Court, that really it seemed quite to belong to the poor woman."

"And what was it?" asked Euphemia.

"The Vampire," said Sir Felix abruptly, and there was a dead pause. Mrs. Blackstone looked at her daughter, and the latter turned very pale.

"I wish," murmured she, looking down, and playing with her rings, "that you had not told me, Sir Felix. How extremely horrid."

Sir Felix laughed. It had been a joke of his brother's, he said, and had seemed so exactly to suit the young woman; "though," added he, "I cannot, with truth, say I assented to the likeness from personal experience, only my guests used to say so, and Lady Mary used to scold my brother for drawing such a comparison for her favourite."

"Ah! then she *was* a favourite?"

"Oh! certainly she was. They could do nothing without her. As for Lady Merivale—my dear Euphemia, you have never seen the Countess, but I hope some day you will—I cannot think how she ever came to part with her, even to Lady Mary; still less can I guess why, when Lady Mary died, she did not go back to her old mistress; for, I assure you, it was a standing joke amongst us all, down at Bohun, that old Lady Merivale must fall to pieces were it not for the vampire!"

Euphemia was curious to know the reason. She was not much used to society—not used at all to the society of venerable grandees, compelled, by their position, to live on the face of the world, and to make the best of their appearance. What did Sir Felix mean by Lady Merivale's falling to pieces?

"Because, my Euphemia"—and the baronet looked at his charming and unsophisticated piece of innocence with delighted eyes—"there never was any one, living and breathing, so completely made up as that old lady. My brother had a curious story about her."

"Your brother seems fond of odd names and stories," said Euphemia, rather pertly.

"He is very quaint and original," smiled Sir Felix; "you will be charmed with him, my dear Euphemia."

"And what was his curious story?" inquired the young lady, evasively.

"Oh, excellent! He happened to be staying at Lord Merivale's once when there was an alarm of fire in the Castle. The galleries were filled with smoke, and the rooms were filled with guests, who all flew down to the great hall in any attire they could find, but strange to say the Countess was nowhere to be seen. Lady Mary was in hysterics, shrieking for her mother, and imploring every one to save her; whilst all the time the old lady was standing in the midst of them, not daring to confess herself, since not one of the twenty people, who sat with her every day at dinner, had an idea that there, in beauty un-adorned, shorn of all her fair proportions, and minus all her 'substitutions,' as Guy used to call them, stood the Countess of Merivale herself!"

"And how did it end?" said Euphemia, quite angrily.

"By the vampire's carrying her off in triumph, and declaring the next morning that her ladyship had escaped to the cellars before any of the house-hold had heard the alarm given!"

"Ha!" exclaimed Mr. Blackstone, speaking for the first time after an hour's devoted attention to the conversation, "how fearful to be thus at the mercy of a dependant! of how many secrets these people often possess themselves, and what fatal use they might make of the power with which the possession invests them! I remember, in days gone by, my old mother used to say......"

"Oh, papa!" laughed Euphemia.

"Yes, my dear; my old mother used to say, no tyranny like the tyranny of a servant."

"And I can believe it, though I never experienced it," said Sir Felix; "at the same time, all this casts no reflection on Ponsford."

"Mamma," said the young lady, as she went up stairs, with her arm round her mother's waist, when the evening closed, "I have a certain conviction, though I never saw him and know nothing of him, that I shall *hate* Mr. Bohun!"

CHAPTER III.

TURN we now to another scene, a fairer scene
than the suburban villa, in spite of its nineteenth-
century-elevation, and all its modern improvements; gaze now, ye eyes that love the old
baronial halls of England, on that large, straggling
pile of buildings, gray with age and green with
ivy, and see what a grand old house Sir Felix
Bohun called his home.

Here and there a turret; here and there a
projection; windows of all sorts and all sizes;
and the whole surrounded by a broad gravel
terrace, from the centre of which sloped a broad
flight of stone steps; then another gravel terrace,
and another flight of steps; a third gravel terrace,
and one last flight of steps—these leading to a
wide park, studded with groups of trees, sheep
under some, and deer under others; and the grass
pressed down into little narrow paths, not meant

to be paths at all, but short cuts to different distant points, too pleasant and convenient for either Sir Felix or Mr. Bohun to do away with.

This was the back of Bohun Court. The entrance was on the gloomy side of the house, looking to the north; and there the stone court-yard, and the stone lions-rampant, and the massive iron-bound oaken door, kept up all the dignity of a baronial hall.

But to turn to the sunny side. On a bright, fresh morning, in early spring, when the sun's rays fell so warmly on the breakfast-room that its long windows were open, a gentleman stepped out on the terrace, with an open letter in his hand, and looked anxiously across the park, as if watch-ing for an expected visitor.

He had not to look long, for, taking advantage of one of the above-mentioned short cuts, another figure was soon seen emerging from an avenue of chesnuts, and wending its way along one of the little beaten tracks.

Mr. Bohun stood still and watched it advancing. As it approached nearer, his eyes seemed to wan-der to the landscape, and rest almost lovingly on its beauty. The haze of a spring morning, and an easterly breeze, was spread like a gauze veil over hill and dale, and over the Bohun woods,

though the dark tops of the fir trees peeped out
here and there, and the wavy outline of distant
downs became every moment more and more
distinct.

Mr. Bohun stood without his hat, and on his
forehead, high and somewhat bald, could be
counted many more wrinkles than even the eyes
of an enemy would have detected on that of Sir
Felix. It was a face of extreme gentleness and
benevolence; but though nature had given him a
five years advantage of his brother in point of
youth, every one would have said the ages were
reversed, and pronounce in favour of Sir Felix,
for Mr. Bohun looked care-worn and old.

All his life long, Mr. Bohun had been the
working brother, and Sir Felix the man of the
gay world, born for society and pleasure, and
carefully avoiding all the worries of every-day
existence. Since these worries must fall to the
lot of some one person in a family, even if not to
all the members, it so happened that destiny had
laid them on the shoulders of Mr. Bohun. He
managed the estate, hired the servants, heard the
grievances, paid the bills, and would have laid
down his life (metaphorically) for Bohun Court,
so it was a labour of love, though a labour all the
same.

And yet there had been two Lady Bohuns?—
Yes. The first a fine lady, who looked upon the
venerable house as a retreat for a fortnight at
Easter and a few months in winter, and hated it
all the rest of the year. The unobtrusive useful-
ness of Mr. Bohun gave her no sort of concern;
it was nothing to her, except that it left Sir Felix
at liberty to spend the springs in London and the
summers abroad with her. Consequently, during
her reign, he was acknowledged and authorised
regent. Even down to the village children, more
hats were doffed to Mr. Bohun than ever little
ragged brims were pulled to Sir Felix.

Then came the second Lady Bohun. She was
a confirmed invalid. Wealth and beauty had been
hers, but health had been denied her. To her
Mr. Bohun was the most devoted of brothers.
Sir Felix was invariably kind and good to her,
but in her state of health she could not tie him
down to Bohun Court—it was so dull for him—
all very well when the house was full of company,
for the hunting season, for instance, or for the
pheasants; but in the dull season, when he had
always been accustomed to gad about, she would
not, for worlds, condemn him to a quietude
which depressed him—no; he should go and
amuse himself.

"Guy and I will keep house; we shall do very
well; and you will come back and refresh us with
all the news, which will suit us far better than
entering into the gaiety ourselves."

And so the regency went on during all the
lingering years of the second Lady Bohun's fragile
existence, and to her Mr. Bohun was the greatest
of comforts, her counsellor, her almoner, her companion, and her friend.

Day by day, all day long if she liked, Mr.
Bohun was at her beck and call to take her orders
and do her commissions, light as air as they always
were!—to walk by the side of her garden chair,
and guide its diminutive pony through the paths
to all her favourite flower beds, or else to the
doors of the cottages which she regularly visited.
It was his study, his happiness, and his pastime to
make those suffering years pass as pleasantly to
her as possible; and when, at last, the garden
chair became too great an exertion, and Lady
Bohun was reduced to her sofa, the very lawn in
front of her morning room was cut up and laid
out under *her* directions and *his* superintendence,
that to the last she might inhale the fragrance she
so loved, and die in the midst of her favourite
occupations; and this, in fact, she did, and Sir
Felix became this time, in reality, a disconsolate
widower.

And Mr. Bohun, did he not miss her? Yes! every hour of his busy day; for, whilst Sir Felix went abroad for change and consolation, *he* remained at his post, haunted by her presence, and living to execute, to the utmost of his power, every wish that she had ever expressed when the scene was closing to her.

And now people really looked upon Mr. Bohun as safe. He had been heir presumptive (not heir presumptuous) for five-and-forty years; now they said he might surely be called heir apparent, and not a voice in all the country round but cordially exclaimed they hoped it might be so. In fact, Sir Felix himself had given it out he never intended to marry again; and he went abroad, and ran the gauntlet of every sort of temptation, and came home again still free, resolved to settle down at Bohun Court, and share with his brother the care of an estate which the love of his lost wife had hallowed.

Business, however, connected with his possessions, took him up to town. Now let us go back to the figure advancing towards Mr. Bohun with outstretched hands, the figure of a gray-haired man, his long locks streaming in the air, a set colour in his thin, worn cheeks, and a white neck-cloth to betoken his vocation.

c 5

"My dear friend, my dear Mr. Bohun! I have made all the haste I possibly could; and my anxiety has given wings to my feet. I see a letter in your hand—confirmation or refutation? Tell me, in a word, is the rumour true?"

The panting breathlessness of the speaker drew a hearty laugh from Mr. Bohun.

"Perfectly true," said he, cheerfully; "and five pages, four of them crossed, full of excuses, which are perfectly unnecessary from my brother, inasmuch as I had no possible right to demand them, no more than I wish him to make them. The rumour is quite true. Sir Felix is really going to be married again, and this is the announcement."

Mr. Bohun held up the letter, and the Rector of Bohun sat down on a bench, overpowered by his feelings.

"I did not think it, I would not believe it," said he, at last, as he flourished his pocket handkerchief in the air; "and I said to my wife, this very morning, Mary, no one but Mr. Bohun shall tell me of it!"

"And Mr. Bohun himself tells you, my good friend," said the heir presumptive, descending from his temporary pedestal with all the equanimity of his character; "indeed, I am not

knocked down by the blow, not half so much as
you appear yourself! cheer up, and remember
that twice before this has happened, and each
time I have been so fortunate as not to be separated from you. It is only the old story over
again!"

"Yes, but the risk, the risk!" ejaculated the
old clergyman, shaking his head; "who knows
what revolution the step may occasion? My dear
friend, if we lost you, what should we do? How
can we spare you if circumstances should require
you to give us less of your personal and moral
support?"

"Twice before the same risk has been run,"
said Mr. Bohun, "and still here I am amongst
you. Twice before I have played the part of a
brother to my brother's wife, and I see no just
cause why my third essay should prove less successful than hitherto."

"Ah! my dear sir," persisted the old clergyman, "it is, as I said before, the risk! the risk!
and at Sir Felix's time of life, too! Dear me!
who would have thought it?"

"I," said Mr. Bohun, firmly; "and I always
have thought it—that my brother was not the
man to settle down quietly as a widower. As for
his time of life, he is still what the world would

call a young man; that is to say, a middle-aged
man; and middle-aged men, my dear Mr. Melville, do not approve of being put on the shelf
merely because they happen to be widowers."

But Mr. Melville was not to be consoled. He
had made up his mind, in common with all the
neighbourhood, that Bohun Court was never
again to see a Lady Bohun—a Mrs. Bohun would
have been welcomed as a novelty; but to see Sir
Felix bring home another bride, and to have to
" make her acquaintance," as the saying is, was a
trial of fortitude.

" And then for it all to happen so suddenly !"
continued Mr. Melville; "it really came upon us
like a thunderbolt, this rumour."

" Rumour, with her many tongues, pointed
them all at Bohun Court," laughed Mr. Bohun,
seemingly resolved to turn the whole affair into
rather a pleasant occurrence than anything else;
" but the singular part of it all is, that, for once
in a way, rumour has hit upon the truth."

" But how did it happen ? Had you any idea
when Sir Felix went up to town? How did this
young lady, if it is a young lady, contrive to
make so sudden an impression?" were a few
amongst the numerous questions which poured
from the lips of the anxious Rector of Bohun.

"Sit down a moment by my side," said Mr. Bohun, leading the old gentleman to a rustic bench on the grass under one of the clumps of old elms; "sit down, and hear the very small cause from which this great event sprung. In the first place, you must know, that my brother went to town on money matters; that it was absolutely necessary he should see his man of business without half an hour's delay; that not finding him at his office, he pursued him all over the City, and on returning late in despair to his office, found he had just left it for good, and had started for the station; you must also know, by the way, that this happy man of business possesses a villa in the suburbs with quite a reputation for beauty and luxury. But to proceed: guess the small cause of this new phase in the destiny of Sir Felix!"

"My dear friend, I am all attention; but I never could guess in all my life—not even the riddle about the first nail in the ark, which every young lady makes a point of asking me in compliment to my cloth—much less can I guess to what you are leading."

"Well, then, the small cause was this, the stopping of my brother's watch! A clerk happened to be just leaving the office as Sir Felix

drove up; he announced that Mr. Blackstone had
just driven off, that he always went home to dinner, that he always dined and slept at The
Laurels. Now this was a delay which might have
put my brother to the greatest inconvenience,
and, in fact, somehow or other, he *must* see Mr.
Blackstone that night, and so it struck him that
the best thing he could do would be to follow
him down to the station—it was merely an interview of a few minutes that was required—he
might catch him before he started. At what
time did he go? At 5·45. Sir Felix looked
at his watch, and jumped into the first Hansom.
He reached the station exactly as the first gate was
being closed, and saw Mr. Blackstone rushing
towards the carriages. To rush after him, and to
spring into a vacant seat by his side, was the
work of a moment—in another he was steaming
towards The Laurels......"

"Well, then, the watch had not stopped?" exclaimed Mr. Melville.

"We have not come to that," returned Mr.
Bohun; "we must now only imagine ourselves
walking up the hill to this suburban villa, Sir
Felix laughing at the adventure, and Mr. Blackstone pressing him to stay and dine, assuring him
that there was a train back again at a quarter

after nine o'clock, which would just suit him; and
so the unbidden guest remained, and was presented to Mrs. Blackstone, and last, not least, to
Miss Blackstone, and it seems that the charms
and accomplishments of the latter—for I am told
she sings like any nightingale—made the two
hours pass like two minutes, although my brother
affirms most seriously that he never had an
idea of losing that 9·15 train. At twenty minutes before nine he looked at his watch, and as
Miss Blackstone had just began another song, he
calculated that he could hear it out, and then he
slily looked at it again. It seems the beauty of
the singer and her song had completely put out of
his head the hour at which the hands had pointed
when he looked last, for seeing they now indi-
cated a quarter to nine, he calmly and gratefully
took his leave, intending to walk down to the
station with his host. Mr. Blackstone seemed
fidgetty, and remarked that they must walk fast;
but my brother assured him there was no hurry,
and persisted in taking his time. The consequence was, that when they reached the station
all was silent. We are much too soon, said Sir
Felix. We have lost the train, thought Mr.
Blackstone, and so it proved. That night my
brother slept at The Laurels, and spent the

greater part of the next day there. This was his
first visit, but not his last by many and many.
The result of these visits you know. He an-
nounces it in this letter, and says he is coming
down here next week to make a few necessary
arrangements."

Mr. Bohun paused, and both he and the Rector
sat in silence for some time, each fully occupied
with his own thoughts.

" Then the lady is handsome," said Mr. Melville, at last.

" So my brother says."

" And shall you go to the wedding ?"

" I conclude my brother will wish it."

" And afterwards ?"

" Oh! return home, I suppose, and get ready
for them. There is so much to be done here before the old house can be made fit for the reception of a gay young bride. The best rooms have
not been opened for more than two years, and we
have let dust and mould gather a good deal about
cherished relics, which, I conclude, had better
now be swept away......"

" Memories and all ?" sighed Mr. Melville.

" Ah! no; never the memories !" exclaimed
Mr. Bohun; " were fifty Lady Bohuns to succeed
the last in this old house, _her_ memory would live in

it, and *her* presence haunt it, just as if her spirit were permitted to return and remind me that though lost, she need not be forgotten."

" I hope it may be so," said the old clergyman, " and I hope past habits and customs and memories may all be retained by the lady whom Sir Felix has chosen."

"I do not doubt it," said Mr. Bohun, rising, " because I believe my brother incapable of selecting any one so devoid of good feeling and good taste as to harbour that most pitiful of human weaknesses, jealousy of the dead."

CHAPTER IV.

Mr. Bohun felt rather nervous and fidgetty the day that Sir Felix was expected down at Bohun Court; and as whatever Mr. Bohun felt, was always felt by the whole household, no one seemed able to settle to anything that day. It was a positive relief when the hoofs of the carriage horses were heard clattering into the court-yard, and Sir Felix's heavy tread sounded in the hall, for then it was over.

There was an awkwardness on both sides when the brothers met, but most on the side of Sir Felix. Mr. Bohun's grasp of the hand was warm and hearty, but his brother's eyes met his with an anxious look, as if to say, had they dared, " Have I made a fool of myself?"

No such accusation, however, welcomed him. The same open, frank cordiality which was Mr. Bohun's characteristic, did not fail him now, and when the first few hours were over—the hours of explanations almost amounting to apologies—the brothers once more stood on precisely the same footing towards each other as ever, with only one slight difference, which was, that it seemed to both as if years, and not weeks, had elapsed since last they parted, the great intervening circumstance appearing to fill up so large a space of time.

To any casual observer, it would have seemed next to absurd to talk of putting Bohun Court in order for the reception of the new guest, so well appointed were all the stately rooms; but Mr. Bohun soon found that his brother had not returned in the same contented state of mind in which he had left home. The "best rooms," as the old housekeeper so proudly called them, were now ordered to be opened, and one bright morning, followed by this ancient servant and Mr. Bohun, Sir Felix made the tour of inspection. But in vain did the old lady expatiate on the carpets, and turn up the corners of the chintz covers, to show how handsome the yellow satin looked underneath. Sir Felix grumbled—the sun happened unfortunately to be shining brightly, and the bridegroom elect made no allowance for the dust and cobwebs of two years' seclusion from light—he called the carpets faded, and the yellow

satin gaudy, and whispered to Mr. Bohun that
" *She* detested yellow—she wished the drawing-
rooms to be crimson."

" Then you will be obliged to have new carpets
—these will not look well with crimson," said his
brother, inwardly marvelling the while at the pre-
mature interest exhibited by the future mistress
of the house.

" True—so we shall," replied Sir Felix com-
posedly, and from the drawing-rooms, he went on
to the dining-room, then to the bedrooms, then to
the attics, and descended the stairs exclaiming, to
the intense mortification of Mrs. Dance, the housekeeper, " All very dingy—there must be a thorough
clean out, and clear out too."

And it was not Mrs. Dance alone who was
mortified at the remarks and behaviour of her
master—it was not she alone who looked and
listened, surprised and dismayed: his brother,
who followed in silence, was no less struck with
the metamorphose in Sir Felix than herself, and
more than once his astonishment nearly found
utterance in the Shakespearian exclamation,
" Thou art translated !"

Yes, Sir Felix *was* translated.   He was a new
man, with certainly a new pair of eyes, for Bohun
Court was no longer fair in his sight, the rooms

no longer grand and stately, the furniture no
longer handsome—everything was dingy !

Dingy ! Mr. Bohun could hardly believe his
ears. · Dingy ! with what then could he be men-
tally comparing it?

Poor Mr. Bohun. What could he know about
it ? what could a vegetating bachelor know of
modern improvements? of carpets in which your
feet were buried—of chairs where you might
sleep a night through, so roomy and so luxurious
—of curtains which looked like the costly twilled
silk of a lady's dress, and which perhaps our
great great grandmothers would have worn as
one—in, short, what could *he* know of comfort,
luxury, and taste, who had never seen even the
outside of the suburban villa, or heard the name
and fame of The Laurels?

And now the survey of the whole house had
been taken, all save one room, and it was with a
visible shrinking that Sir Felix saw Mrs. Dance
single out a key tied with a bow of red ribbon,
and turn it in the lock.

This was a small room unconnected with the
suite of drawing-rooms, library, and dining-room.
It was at the southern side of the house, and looked
upon a flower garden cut into innumerable beds,
excepting just under the wide bay-window, and

there there was a broad border in which were all
the clusters of violets and lilies of the valley.
Climbing up the window was a passion flower,
throwing out its long creepers amongst the nailed-
up branches of a luxuriant jessamine, and here
and there a tuft of that curious brown stock which
only exhales its exquisite scent at night.

They were now in this room, and Mr. Bohun
walked hastily to the window the moment they
entered. Sir Felix stood still, and looked round
without uttering a syllable. This was a room
filled with innumerable relics of the past. This
was the last Lady Bohun's own boudoir, where
she had spent all her latest hours. On that sofa
she had passed the suffering time; in that chair,
when breath was failing her, had she been placed
by Mr. Bohun, and breathed her last sigh upon
his cheek. On the grass under that window, were
still the four patches worn away by the wheels of
her garden chair.

Suddenly Mr. Bohun turned. " You will have
nothing touched here?" said he to his brother, in
a tone partly of entreaty, partly interrogatory.
" You need not," he continued, seeing that Sir
Felix hesitated. " This is a very small room—it
will not be wanted—it does not interfere with the
suite—the octagon room between the drawing-

rooms will make a perfect lady's boudoir. Do not touch *this* room, Felix !"

Sir Felix gulped down a feeling that rose in his throat, and turned away.

"Do what you like here," said he, with an effort; "take it as your own, Guy. You have a natural affection for the room, and you deserve to appropriate it. Remember, Mrs. Dance, that should Mr. Bohun be absent when the workmen come down to do up the house, the key is to be turned upon that room, and no step but my brother's enter within that door."

Mrs. Dance curtsied low, and looking at Mr. Bohun, coloured tearfully, as Sir Felix strode away.

"I'm glad, sir," said she, in a faltering voice, "I'm very glad Sir Felix gives up this room to you. I was so afraid it was to be all new done like the rest. Is there anything you would please to have altered, sir?"

No; Mr. Bohun gave the strictest injunctions on this point. Not a chair, nor a table, nor an ornament was to be moved.

"I shall bring down a few things from my den upstairs, Mrs. Dance—just my books, and my stuffed birds, and some of the pictures—perhaps I shall bring everything. Yes—I think you

may possess yourself of my den, Mrs. Dance, and
make a lumber room of it.   I like this room—I
love it—it is my whole home, and here I shall
live, and be in nobody's way.   Mrs. Dance, if you
bring any paint, and paper, and whitewashing into
it, I never will forgive you.   I think you understand me ?"

"Oh, sir !" exclaimed the old lady, tottering
away; "trust me, trust me.   I understand you
perfectly; I feel as you do yourself."

So now the worst was over, except the final
conversation between Sir Felix and Mr. Bohun,
as to whether the latter should continue to make
Bohun Court his home.   Mr. Bohun urged that
such an arrangement might not be agreeable, and
hinted at chambers in the Albany.   Sir Felix
scouted the idea, and declared that Bohun Court
could not go on without his brother, and the argument raged fiercely till the bridegroom conquered,
and the bachelor gave way.

And when this was settled all seemed smooth.
Sir Felix started for London, and Mr. Bohun was
to follow in a week, to see and be presented to the
bride elect, and become acquainted with her.   The
newly married couple were then to go abroad, and
Mr. Bohun was to return home to make ready for
their reception when they came back towards
autumn.

CHAPTER V.

TIME had now arrived to within a few days of the wedding. Mr. Blackstone had got through the elaborate settlements which had made his daughter mistress of forty thousand pounds, independent of her expectations; and Mrs. Blackstone had achieved the *trousseau*, and seen it all laid out for exhibition. The bride was in a great state of excitement, arranging affairs of much greater importance—namely, the procession of the brides-maids, and their programme of behaviour. Also, Ponsford was in full force, regularly installed as lady's maid, and doing the honours of the millinery and jewellery with great effect. All Mrs. Black-stone's circle were very much awed and impressed with her manners on the occasion, and even Euphemia allowed herself to be guided by her in every respect.

"Ponsford," she exclaimed, running into her

room early one morning, " put me out something
very smart.   We are going to spend the day at
the Crystal Palace, and Mr. Bohun is to see me
there for the first time.   What had I better
wear?"

" Not anything very smart, ma'am," was
Ponsford's reply, " if you wish to make a fa-
vourable impression on Mr. Bohun."

Euphemia's clear blue eyes grew into a circle.

" Why?" she exclaimed; " is he so very
difficult to please?   A man of his age !"

" Oh, ma'am !" said the maid, with a smile,
" he may not be a very young gentleman; but I
have heard the ladies at Bohun Court say they
were more particular about their dress when Mr.
Bohun was at home, than when they dressed for
London dinners in the season."

Euphemia bit her lips and pouted.

" Do you think he really is a judge?"

" Oh, yes, ma'am ! that I *know*."

" What style of people—I mean dress—does he
admire?"

Ponsford began first by describing what she
imagined to be Mr. Bohun's style of beauty,
and did it so adroitly that Euphemia looked in
the glass with a proud smile on her lips.   She
flattered herself the difficult man would have

little fault to find with his brother's taste in *that* respect !

Meanwhile, her maid was spreading out a very handsome light brown silk dress, of a shade approaching fawn.

"Oh, Ponsford !" cried the young lady, "not that quakerish thing ! I mean that for country walks in the dust and the mud. Give me the Eugénie blue for to-day."

"Miss Blackstone, this pale brown, with your Spanish mantilla, and that lovely lilac crape bonnet which came last night, would, I assure you, be in better taste for the occasion than the bright blue."

"Why ?" exclaimed Euphemia, firing up. " I should think I knew pretty well what ought to be worn at the Crystal Palace !"

" Of course, ma'am," replied Ponsford, hastily. "I did not mean that. I meant considering your present position, ma'am ; and also, since you rather wished, I thought, to wear something according to Mr. Bohun's taste. Engaged young ladies," she added, seeing a frown gathering on Euphemia's brow, " always attract so much attention."

" So they do," interrupted the bride elect; "so perhaps, after all, I had better look rather quiet than otherwise. Very well. I will wear the brown silk. That gorgeous mantilla will set it off. Do you know, Ponsford, that Sir Felix gave forty guineas for that mantilla?"

"I dare say, ma'am. I know they are very expensive."

"How do you know? I thought they were very rare. Sir Felix said so."

"So they are, as handsome as this, ma'am."

"Do you know how to put it on, Ponsford?"

"Oh, yes, ma'am!"

"Are you sure? Because Sir Felix said there was a particular way."

"I know quite well, ma'am."

"But how do you know so well?"

"Lady Mary wore one constantly, ma'am."

"Oh!" Miss Blackstone was satisfied. And then she continued, "But, Ponsford, about Mr. Bohun—is he like Sir Felix?"

"Not the least, ma'am. Mr. Bohun looks much older; more like a country gentleman, too. He has quite a different sort of manner and voice, and he has a very decided way of speaking."

"Good looking?"

"Not so handsome as Sir Felix, ma'am."

"I wonder why he never married?"

"I cannot say, ma'am. I never heard of his

paying any lady attention. Lady Mary used to
say he was the most unsusceptible person she
ever met. Besides, ma'am, he is so comfortable
at Bohun Court."

" But that cannot be like his own home," said
Euphemia. " By the by, I wonder where his
own home is?"

" Bohun Court, ma'am," said Ponsford, slightly
pinching in her lips.

There was a pause. A red flush came over
Euphemia's face, and she paused in the operation
of pulling out a bow with her bonnet strings.
The flush heightened to a glow. Something was
stirring in her mind, and she breathed quicker
than before. Ponsford was deeply engrossed with
the folding of the Spanish mantilla.

How was it that that " something " had never
stirred in Euphemia's mind before ? " How was
it," thought she to herself, "that I never dreamt
of asking Sir Felix if Mr. Bohun always lived at
Bohun Court ? Perhaps he does not: I shall not
like it if he does. I always thought Sir Felix
had no 'encumbrances' (as Fanny Washington
calls relations) about the house. I must find it
all out. I remember, when the Washingtons
came to congratulate, Mrs. Washington particularly said how completely I should be mistress

at Bohun Court, just as if Sir Felix had been a
bachelor; but if I am to have a fidgetty, difficult
man always watching me, planted there for life
(for evidently he is a regular old bachelor), I
shall not like it at all. I'll ask Sir Felix cleverly
—perhaps Mr. Bohun only comes for the country
seasons—if I don't like him, I can coax Sir Felix
up to town at those times; at all events, I'll
sound Sir Felix this very day."

By this time the mantilla was ready. It was
placed over the graceful shoulders after the most
approved fashion, and Euphemia descended to the
drawing-room.

There was one difference between the feelings
with which she descended the staircase, and
those with which she had mounted them. *Then*
she said Mr. Bohun was to see her for the first
time; *now* she felt that she was going to see
him.

"Well!" exclaimed Mrs. Blackstone, as her
daughter entered the room, "I do think, my
dear, that is the very prettiest bonnet I ever saw.
But, surely, you are very plainly dressed? I
should have thought that lovely blue silk would
have been more the thing?"

"Ponsford said not, mamma;" replied the young
lady, whose temper had received a shock a few

minutes before, and had not recovered; "Ponsford said it was too smart for the occasion."

" Too smart? good gracious, dear child! when I declare I have seen the Duchess of —— there in almost a ball-dress!"

" Perhaps so, mamma, but Ponsford knows so perfectly what people ought to wear; she meant that *in my position* I ought not to make such a show, and my dress is very handsome though it is quiet."

At that instant wheels were heard on the gravel, and Sir Felix sprang out of the basket carriage, with its two spirited little ponies, in which he was to have the privilege of driving Miss Blackstone to Sydenham.

No sooner had he entered the room, than Mrs. Blackstone called his attention to her daughter's Spanish mantilla.

" Does it not look magnificent, Sir Felix?—is it not becoming?"

" Yes," was his reply, as his eyes took a gratified survey of the lady of his choice; "but we must not bestow all the praise on the mantilla. It is a pleasure to give Euphemia anything pretty, for she does such credit to it. Her whole dress to-day is *fait-à-peindre*."

The young girl laughed, but gave her mother

a sly glance at the same time. It was Ponsford's taste, and Ponsford's triumph; and whilst the daughter was simply pleased at it, the mother was silent from feeling obliged, somewhat reluctantly, to acknowledge it.

A large party went in Mrs. Blackstone's suite to the Crystal Palace that day. She had engaged a room for thirty, instead of disarranging The Laurels before the wedding, when a still larger number of friends were invited to breakfast.

Amongst the most intimate of these friends ranked the Washingtons, very wealthy people of the same sphere as the Blackstones.

Mrs. Washington had several daughters, and Fanny, with a younger sister, were to be two of the bridesmaids. It was Fanny for whom Miss Blackstone had laughingly promised to send, should she find that Mr. Bohun was "worth having." It was, consequently, Fanny, who, on this day of the grand Crystal Palace party, was in agonies (to use her own forcible expression) to see her probable "*futûr*," so the Washingtons were at the place of rendezvous, by the statue of Cain, long before any one else had arrived.

Some went in carriages, some went on horseback, some by train; but these were chiefly the gentlemen of the party, whose occupations

obliged them to spend their mornings in town.
There was no want of money in that pretty
suburb of London. Houses and carriages all bore
equally the unmistakable stamp of wealth, from
the well-appointed barouche of Mrs. Washington
with its handsome bays, down to Euphemia's own
basket carriage with its soft blue velvet cushions.

And their dress! the costly silks that stood
alone! the pink and blue parasols covered with
real point; the white ones with coral drops all
the way round; the lovely bonnets covered with
real Mechlin! Every one had been anxious to
do honour to that party, and certainly Mrs.
Blackstone's guests did that day make a most
refulgent show.

At last the bride-elect and her intended arrived, the former tired and dusty, although so
muffled up, for fear of the sun and dust, that no
one could have imagined how slender a figure all
those summer wraps concealed, until she emerged
from them.

Fanny Washington came up to her immediately.

" My dear," she whispered, " I have been looking everywhere for a young likeness of Sir Felix,
and can see nobody at all likely."

" I dare say not," said Euphemia, " for every-

body says he looks ten years older;" and her
quick eye ran over the assembled party.

No; certainly there was no one there who
could be Mr. Bohun. She did not like remark-
ing upon his absence to Sir Felix; it was making
his brother of too much importance; besides, she
had been talking conversation to him for two
hours, beating about the bush to find out all she
could without deliberately asking the plain question, "Is Bohun Court his home?" and she was
tired, nervous, too, for there was a little shadow
of annoyance in Sir Felix's manner at some of
her questions which showed her that she was
treading on dangerous ground, so she had learnt
nothing, but, on the contrary, had been obliged
to give the subject up altogether.

"However," thought she, as the party began
now to disperse and look about them, "I shall get
on better with the individual himself when he appears. I shall not be afraid of him."

Meanwhile, as they wandered about, Mrs.
Washington came to walk and talk confidentially
with Mrs. Blackstone. She had married three
daughters herself, and was therefore quite *au fait*
in such matters. She was full of delight at
"dear Phemy's" good fortune and happiness, but
thought her looking rather pale and nervous.

Possibly it was the lilac bonnet, which was always trying, or probably the prospect of being introduced to her future husband's relations. That was always a great trial for a young girl, and she knew from experience how glad all the brides she ever knew were when that part of the ordeal was over.

"But fortunately for dear Phemy," she ran on, and her voice sounded to Mrs. Blackstone like a bee humming in her ear, "fortunately for dear Phemy, Sir Felix has no relations but a brother. I am delighted to hear we are to meet him here to-day. I looked in the Baronetage and saw he was five years younger than Sir Felix, but it did not say if he were in the army or the navy; perhaps he is a barrister?"

Mrs. Blackstone thought not. She believed he was merely a country gentleman. Mrs. Washington was down upon her directly. "Oh! really? then I suppose he has a place of his own: in what county, I wonder?"

Now Mrs. Blackstone, in her own heart, had always had more than a suspicion that Mr. Bohun lived entirely at Bohun Court, and once or twice it had occurred to her that she ought very delicately to insinuate to Sir Felix that if that were the case, Euphemia ought to be officially informed of the fact, and consulted as to whether such an arrangement met her approbation; but somehow or other she had never had courage to attack him on the subject, and, besides, there was always a sort of hauteur about Sir Felix, in spite of his courteous manners, which, to confess the plain truth, kept her at a distance.

But this sort of delicacy and timidity would not have been understood or appreciated by Mrs. Washington. She was one of those maternal martyrs who would sacrifice themselves and everybody else upon the altars dedicated to their daughters, and had she not, before their marriages, arranged everything for the. comfort and happiness of their future homes without regard to the wishes or feelings of her sons-in-law, she would have considered herself most culpable. She feared, as she often said, neither man nor beast; but whether she used the latter term in reference to any of her sons-in-law, it was impossible to say.

No wonder that Mrs. Blackstone dreaded lest her warm friend should, even at the eleventh hour, discover this suspected flaw in the brilliant alliance, and impart it in accents of pity to her ten thousand friends; so she turned off the conversation by saying she had lost sight of Phemy, and that Phemy had made her promise faithfully not to do so, as she wished her to be present at her introduction to Mr. Bohun.

Mr. Bohun was becoming rapidly magnified into a person of immense consequence.

So Mrs. Blackstone hurried after her daughter, and Mrs. Washington looked about for hers. Phemy and Sir Felix were standing arm-in-arm in the gallery, looking over at all the flowering water plants floating on the pure surface of the basins. Fanny Washington had just joined them.

"Phemy, dear," she whispered, as Mrs. Blackstone engaged Sir Felix in conversation on the other side, "I want to know if your inamorato is at all disposed to be jealous?"

"I hope he is," returned Phemy, with a coquettish smile, "but as yet I have never had an opportunity of trying him. Why do you ask?"

"Because there has been a gentleman down there—the oddest-looking man you ever saw, with an odd-shaped hat drawn over his eyes, and his hand over his mouth—he has been standing leaning against that statue for about half-an-hour, watching all your movements."

"I do not see him," said Phemy.

"Follow the direction of my eyes—there—he is moving—he sees us looking at him—he is coming under this gallery to have a better view of you. Oh? Phemy, he is evidently very much struck. Is he not a curious figure?"

"Wait till he comes quite under," laughed Phemy, in a whisper, "and then we will have some fun with him." Phemy held in her hand a bunch of moss rosebuds, and from these she selected a blighted one, dried up into a hard ball. "As he passes beneath," said she, "I will drop this down upon him."

Sir Felix had no great admiration of Miss Washington. He thought she was a frivolous, foolish companion for his peerless Euphemia, and when he heard this whispering, joking conversation going on, he lent an attentive ear to it, and answered all Mrs. Blackstone's remarks at random; but, when he saw the bouquet being taken to pieces, he could refrain no longer, and exclaimed, "You are surely not going to do such a thing?"

He referred to the destruction of the bouquet; he had not heard the previous conversation; but Euphemia thought he meant not going to throw the rosebud over, so she betrayed herself unnecessarily.

"Dear Sir Felix......only our joke......you ought to be quite flattered; there is a gentleman down there, coming towards us now, who has never taken his eyes off me for the last half hour, and we thought that just as he came under this gallery, we would drop this dead rosebud on his hat, and such a hat as it is!"

Sir Felix looked—started—seized Euphemia's hand, and, drawing it through his arm, exclaimed, as he moved quickly away, " How thankful I am you did no such thing! Euphemia, it is my brother!"

CHAPTER VI.

THE wedding was over. The carriages were driving up to The Laurels in rapid succession, and Lady Bohun sat in a chair of state in the drawing-room, looking somewhat pale, nervous, and bewildered as most brides do, but still receiving the congratulations of the numerous friends who crowded round her, with a pleased, happy expression—just perhaps a little touch of pride in her manner—a little assumption of dignity, as if she already felt she had risen a step in the scale of society, and yet could hardly realise it.

One after the other came her friends—some matrons, cheering up the young daughter on leaving her home—some girls, admiring her costly rings, and examining the rich lace about her—others neither girls nor matrons, telling her she was a lucky girl, and that it was not everybody who could catch a rich Baronet without encumbrances.

" And as for his brother, dear Phemy, what a delightful creature ! we have all lost our hearts. There is something about Sir Felix that always rather awes one; Mr. Bohun is charming. Such a kind good face—very like Sir Felix too—but easier to get on with. Ah, you are a lucky girl!"

As yet, Phemy felt very strange with Mr. Bohun. She had not exchanged ten words with him, nor many more looks, so his praises did not call forth any echo, but she felt he was continually watching her. Sir Felix stood amongst a knot of gentlemen, keeping a sly eye on the gravel sweep in hopes of seeing the four greys bring round his new chariot; but Mr. Bohun was hovering near, waiting till he could take advantage of some gap in the circle round her, but this she did not know. She thought he was merely watching, and she chafed under it.

At last there was a vacant space and he stepped in, bent over the orange blossoms, and spoke to her.

" At last I have found an opportunity of wishing my new sister every joy and happiness." Phemy bowed and smiled. " It is late in the day to do so, but that has not been for want of the will, but the way ; you have had quite a bevy round you."

"Yes—so many friends."

Phemy did not know what else to say. To everybody else she had had answers and lively repartees ready, but there was something about Mr. Bohun that made her silent against her will, for in her heart, she was longing to talk to him. She felt that she neither liked nor admired him as all the rest of the room did, but she would not have had any one suspect it for the world. She would not allow any soul to suspect that there was the faintest cloud in the horizon of her happiness, or the slightest tarnish on the brilliancy of her triumph.

This was Lady Bohun's peculiar kind of pride— peculiar to herself, and yet common enough amongst worldlings.

Was there ever a large circle of acquaintance, amongst whom, when a brilliant match was announced, some were not found who studiously set to work to pick a hole in the fortunes, or the families, of the bridegroom or the bride? Do not people talk on the occasion somewhat as follows?

"Have you heard that Caroline A. is going to be very well married?"

"Yes—that is to say if you call it very well, when I don't suppose they can muster twelve hundred a year between them; and as for *him*, poor man, though he is an honourable, he is perfectly deaf in one ear."

Or else,

" That handsome Sir Henry B. is actually going to be married at last. Miss C. is a lucky girl— her parents are delighted, and he has seven thousand a year if he has a shilling."

" I dare say he has; but don't you remember an odd story about him some years ago? All the world knew it then, though perhaps it may be hushed up now, and he did not get out of it very well either."

So much for the bridegrooms, and the brides fare but little better.

" Good gracious! Mr. D. going to marry Lotty Eversfield. Is the day fixed? then I hope she will not change her mind before it arrives! a good match for her? Yes—any match is good for such a finished coquette, and I am sure her mother must be thankful to have her settled."

Or else,

" Colonel E.'s daughter is engaged to Mr F., who owns that lovely place down in Yorkshire. Nothing can be more suitable than the match; he has wealth and a princely estate, and she has youth and beauty."

"Youth? oh, my dear friend, I remember her before she could run alone. She must be eight-and-twenty, if she is a day."

"Pardon me—her own mother told me she was of age last birthday."

"My dear, in the first place, own mothers are the last people to be believed, when a daughter's age is in question, and in the next, I know she is eight-and-twenty for a fact. Have you ever seen her?"

"No, but I know him well."

"She is no beauty. She has certainly a very fine complexion, and if you could give yourself the trouble, you might have the same; that's all *I* have to say."

And so on in every case without an exception. The world does not allow of the existence of such a thing as an unexceptionable match on both sides. There never was a marriage yet that *somebody* did not try to depreciate, and, to return to our subject, this the new made Lady Bohun well knew. It was therefore her particular pride to be able to say, "There is no skeleton in *my* house!"

Mr. Bohun returned to the charge. "I think my brother told me you had never been abroad?"

"Never—that is, only to Dieppe."

"You will be delighted with Paris."

" So I believe. I hear the shops are lovely."

" But with the buildings."

" Ah, I don't care for buildings. I am told the shops are so tempting, that I shall hope to pick up a great many pretty things."

" Then," said Mr. Bohun smiling, " I expect you will transform Bohun Court quite into a temple of the graces."

Euphemia turned her eyes quickly on him.

" Is it a very old fashioned place?" said she.

" Not very modern—you will see 1615 carved in the stonework over the entrance; but do you know we are very proud of that date? we don't despise Bohun Court because of its antiquity."

This was said laughingly, but the " we" sounded unpleasantly on Lady Bohun's ears. She felt she did not like it, though she tried to conceal the feeling, and carry it off, so that he should not perceive it, so she answered—

" Of course not, but I meant about the furniture; I suppose all that is rather—rather—ancient, is it not?"

" It was, but a complete renovation is going on. I hope, by your return, everything will be to your taste and in apple-pie order. I only know it shall not be my fault if it is not."

" When are you going down?" asked Euphemia, her heart beginning to beat quicker.

" To-night," said Mr. Bohun, innocently.

Now was the moment.

" Do you always live at Bohun Court ?"

It was out at last, and Mr. Bohun seemed struck with something in her voice as she asked the question. He looked at her—she was very pale, but that she was before; had he not looked at her he would have answered readily " yes," but now— he modified the reply : " Hitherto I have done so," said he, and there was a dead pause.

Fortunately it was but of a moment's duration, for Sir Felix had espied the greys coming round, and he crossed the room to where his brother stood.

" You must let Euphemia go," said he, " for the carriage will soon be here. The horses have arrived."

And Euphemia was carried off by her mamma and the bridesmaids.

" Are you pleased ?" whispered Sir Felix.

" She is beautiful," replied Mr. Bohun.

" But you, my dear fellow, you must be bored to death."

" Not at all. I assure you I have been vastly amused. I sat by an old lady at breakfast who paid me immense attention. She questioned me most narrowly as to my birth, parentage, and education—almost as to my prospects."

"Mrs. Washington! that imperial pumpkin, as I always call her. The most indefatigable of match makers and manœuverers. Ah, Guy, I shall be glad to withdraw Euphemia from this set—she is worth better things."

"Any parting commands for me?"

"No, no, I think not. I will write if anything occurs to me. Leave all the tables and chairs at Bohun as they are. Perhaps we may be tempted with some furniture in Paris, and if so, it will only be money thrown away to make additions at present."

Up-stairs the bride was attiring for her journey, tremulous, and very silent. The tearful mother, seated sobbing by her side and unable even to look at the adornment of her darling, attributed this nervous taciturnity to the young girl's efforts at self-command, but, could any eye have peeped into the recesses of that heart, they would have read a different story—a story that told of the blot on the brightness of her fate, and her sudden consciousness of the fact. She had just awoke to the conviction that, unless she took great care, there would be a skeleton in her house after all!

But she was Lady Bohun at all events—she felt Lady Bohun every inch—more especially when Ponsford glided up to her with a pair of jewel cases in her hand, and said, as if she had said it all her life, "Which of these bracelets will your ladyship be pleased to wear on the journey?"

Down-stairs, all the guests were crowding into the balcony, or out upon the staircase, to take the last look of the bride. Lower still in the hall, all the servants were ranged to catch her eye, and bid her their farewell. Who does not know all this regular routine of a gay wedding?

It was a grand day for The Laurels, even though Mrs. Blackstone had concealed herself behind the back drawing-room door, and was crying her heart out. It was a grand day, although the elderly couple were left childless, and all that they had lived for was carried off from them by Sir Felix Bohun. It was a grand day for Mr. and Mrs. Blackstone, thought all their guests. They did not see the big tears twinkled away out of the old man's eyes, as he handed his daughter into her new carriage, nor did they guess what it cost him to gulp down the choking in his throat as he re-entered the drawing-room rubbing his hands and smiling convulsively, and, suspecting his wife's hiding-place, trying to draw the crowd away from it, and entice them to the window to see the four grays flying along the dusty road over the common till they turned the corner and disappeared behind the trees.

Nobody saw all this; nobody felt it; for the departure of the bride and bridegroom is a moment of great excitement, and, after that, comes the excitement of trying who can get away first.

But Mrs. Washington clung to her friend—invaded her retreat behind the door, having espied a corner of the gray moiré-antique coming through the crevice—pounced on her like a spider on a fly, and, with all the pertinacity of the most inconvenient friendship, invited herself to dinner to talk it all over.

And the bridesmaids stood in a cluster at one of the open windows making remarks on Mr. Bohun, who, wandering about with a talkative gentleman of whose name he had not the slightest idea, was learning a great many lessons about ornamental gardening down on the lawn beneath, and waiting impatiently for the moment when he could politely take his leave, and say that he had only just time to save the train.

" I like him," said one; " he is not so pompous as Sir Felix."

" I look on him as a dethroned monarch," said Fanny Washington; " mamma found out that he has no home but Bohun Court. Phemy won't

stand that, I suspect. Mamma says she found
out, too, that he has always completely managed
the estate and the household."

"Pleasant for Phemy," exclaimed another;
"Phemy, who made slaves of even those dear old
Blackstones, her own parents!"

"Phemy will make a slave of him, too," said a
fourth.

"He does not look as if he would be a slave,"
chimed in a fifth; "in spite of all that suavity,
there is a very firm cut about his mouth and chin.
Now, Sir Felix is too polished for my taste—too
much of a courtier, or a gentleman of the old
school. Mr. Bohun is so blunt and straightforward; Phemy will never bend *him* to be her
slave."

"Then," said Fanny Washington, "she will
make his residence in the house disagreeable to
him, and so it will come to the same thing in
the end."

"Unless Sir Felix brings down that temper of
hers before she fairly mounts the throne of Bohun
Court," retorted another.

"Which he is not likely to do," was Fanny
Washington's rejoinder, and then the group of her
bosom friends dispersed.

Yes, they were her bosom friends, but never

mind, she could not hear them. She was Phemy Bohun now, on the pinnacle of her prosperity, and on the high road to Dover ; so, of course, her dear friends had a perfect right to say what they pleased of her—behind her back.

If we could all hear what our dear friends say of us behind our backs, how many friends should we go through the world with, and have left to us at the last?

CHAPTER VII.

On the estate of Bohun, about a mile from the house, was a pretty little cottage ornée, occupied by an old lady, long a dependant on the Bohun family. In her youth she had been governess to the mother of the present Sir Felix, who, in her old age, had installed her comfortably in this cottage, rent free.

A passing visit to old Mrs. Trant was one of the almost daily duties of Mr. Bohun's life. It was a habit both he and Sir Felix had got into, from its having been a habit of the late Lady Bohun's, whose garden-chair nearly every day conveyed her to the old lady with the first of the fruits, the flowers, and the vegetables. Mrs. Trant used to say, that the death of this Lady Bohun had been the greatest blow she had ever received! to use her own expression, "it had shaken her on the pedestal of her life."

No wonder, then, that when she heard that Sir Felix was going to try his chance in the great lottery a third time, her anxiety was great as to how far the new successor would come up in perfection to the amiable being who had preceded her.

Perhaps she was anxious on her own account as well as on that of Sir Felix. Almost entirely a prisoner to her cottage from feeble health, it was a matter of no small importance to her as to how far the coming bride would replace the friend she had lost—friend and companion both, had the last Lady Bohun been—and, in addition to this feeling, there was her affection for Sir Felix, an affection of nearly half a century's growth.

Anxiously, then, she waited, the day after the announcement appeared in the *Times*, seated in her sunny little bay window, for the swing of her garden gate, and the firm, heavy tread of Mr. Bohun's foot on the gravel path behind the evergreen hedge which skirted her lawn.

True to his promise he came, the tread, perhaps, not quite so brisk, or the manner quite so gay as usual; but still there he was, faithful to his habit, and once seated in the sunny little corner opposite to her, he soon seemed restored to himself again, and ready to answer all her queries and satisfy her pardonable curiosity.

Naturally enough, there was but one subject of conversation between them, and that, the wedding; not the wedding in its small worldly details, but the wedding as by far the most important event in the life of one dear to them both— the wedding in all its bearings as touching the future happiness or misery of the declining years of a man's life! for neither attempted to conceal from the other that it was late in life for another new tie to be formed, after two had been destroyed.

"Is she a person suited to Sir Felix?" was Mrs. Trant's anxious inquiry; "does she appear likely to make him happy?"

"She is very young—very gay—very pretty," said Mr. Bohun, evading the direct question; "she looks younger still by my brother's side, but as to her more intrinsic qualifications, I only saw her surrounded by friends."

"Is she pleasing?"

Mr. Bohun hesitated. "A bride," said he, "is generally seen to disadvantage, running, for the first time, the gauntlet of her husband's relations. I had only a few moments conversation with her, but you know how difficult Sir Felix is to please, so let us give her credit for great powers that way."

All this was but negative approbation, and Mrs. Trant saw it, though she forbore to remark upon it, and Mr. Bohun continued—

" I do not know if you remember that I have a peculiar theory of my own on the subject of smiles. I think they are more characteristic than frowns—more expressive than words—and Miss Euphemia Blackstone's smile did not hit my fancy; otherwise, she has her full share of beauty, as you will see."

" Do they propose coming down soon? Is she not anxious to see Bohun Court?"

" As if Bohun Court were the 'little bit of heaven dropped on earth' which the poets sing so daintily," laughed Mr. Bohun. " No, they are bound for Italy, and talk of remaining away till September or October."

" She will lose the Bohun woods when the leaves are changing, then," said the old lady, in a tone of commisseration.

" She may not appreciate all these things as we do," returned Mr. Bohun; " remember, she is a town-bred young lady, and never having been abroad, may be too much fascinated by the gaities she will enter into in France and Italy, to wish to settle down in our quiet corner immediately."

Mrs. Trant did not augur favourably of the bride from what she gleaned in this conversation. She had an idea that she was a common-place person.

" But, no," said Mr. Bohun, " my brother would never have tolerated, much less selected, a common-place person. There is a great deal of character about the lady of his choice, but being very young and unformed in manners, I am not prepared to say whether this kind of character tends to good or evil. I should say that she was impressionable, and that Sir Felix may mould her to anything, since she appeared ready enough to give up to him in several little matters connected with their future plans."

" That is a good beginning," remarked the old lady; " trifles show characters sometimes more than great actions. But talking of plans, I take a deep interest in other plans besides those of Sir Felix and his bride. Tell me of yourself, my dear Mr. Guy."

" Myself?" Mr. Bohun did not seem quite to understand. " How do you mean, dear old friend?"

" I mean, does this event change your arrangements at all? Do you still contemplate residing at Bohun Court?"

Mr. Bohun hesitated for some time before he answered.

"Do you know," said he, at last, "that this is a subject to which I know I ought to have given some attention, and I have not done so. Before the marriage, my brother and I had a fierce argument on this very point, and I gave way to his earnest wish that I should remain here to continue to manage affairs as I have always done. Ladies don't take kindly to farm matters, and land cannot well be governed by female heads; so that really, in assenting to his wish that no change should be made, I believed I was acting for his happiness and advantage (if my modesty may permit of my saying so). But now, dear old friend and counsellor, that you have kindly and wisely put it into my head that *I* ought to have plans as well as *they*, why, I think with you, and I humbly crave your advice."

"Dear Mr. Guy, I am not qualified to advise; all depends so entirely on the kind of partner Sir Felix has selected. It was this that made me so minute in my inquiries, for we cannot afford to lose you, and yet......"

" And yet what ?"

" It is not often that the residence of a third person with new married people answers."

"You are quite right. It never occurred to me, but you are perfectly right, and I ought to have given the subject more consideration. As it is, I see nothing for it but just to wait and see how things go on. After my promise to Sir Felix, I could not well upset all the arrangements at this early stage of the new administration. You do not think I could, do you?"

"No," said Mrs. Trant, "but I know your nature. You have hitherto been singularly fortunate."

"You think I shall have difficulties to contend with?"

"It is possible—I hope not probable—but the ground is as yet untried; and, as I said before, these arrangements seldom do answer—every day you see instances of it."

"True," said Mr. Bohun, "and perhaps I have been unwise. I see it, now that it is too late. But then again—the estate!"

In Mr. Bohun's estimation, every consideration was as nothing compared to Bohun Court. His own happiness was bound up in it—his own comfort, a trifle in the balance.

He leant back in his chair in a reverie of mingled feelings. Could it be possible, thought he, that the entrance of a mere girl into the

family could create a revolution which would, in
the most remote degree, affect plans which had
been in undisturbed operation for years? Was it
possible for one so young, so apparently frivolous,
spoilt, half-educated—for Mr. Bohun's penetration
had made all these discoveries during two short
days spent in her presence—one so unfit to rule—
was it possible that *for her* he was to upset the
government of Bohun Court, by withdrawing
himself from a share in it, and thereby put
Sir Felix into a position both of discomfort and
perplexity?

What did Sir Felix know of business?—nothing.
What was he but a highly polished, travelled, accomplished man of the world?—nothing! And
a smile, proud, almost triumphant, curled Mr.
Bohun's firm lip.

"No!" he exclaimed, forgetting that Mrs.
Trant could not have been following his train of
thought, though she could guess it by sympathy;
"there can be no change of plans until a more
rightful heir stands in my shoes. No woman can
displace the male heirs of Bohun Court."

"It is not entailed," said Mrs. Trant, gently.

"Very true," returned Mr. Bohun, hastily;
"and I am glad that you remind me, for it
ought to be, for fear of accidents; and it *shall*

be, at the very first opportunity, even though, by urging it on my brother, I cut my own throat!"

He walked home to Bohun Court hurriedly. He was perturbed. For years and years his unruffled spirit had never been so stirred up as now, and he threaded the woods with a rapid step, seemingly longing to catch sight of his home, even as if a spirit were at his heels making a greedy clutch at the prize, the possession of which depended on the issue of the race between them.

The sun, like a red ball of fire, was just dipping behind the belt of dark woods, which formed a background to the scene, as he crossed the lawn. The grim old mansion looked gray and cold outside, but when he entered, the changes that had taken place, consequent on the marriage of Sir Felix, seemed to strike Mr. Bohun for the first time.

Inside, it was now a mansion of modern days, gay and costly as all the first upholsterers in London could make it. There was the boudoir, glittering in blue satin and white and gold furniture; the drawing-rooms radiant in cherry satin, and velvet carpets with white grounds; the dining-room a perfect triumph of art, for it had been a gloomy room, and was now a gay one.

But everything was gay—everything fit for the bride whom it was destined to welcome and to please. But outside—

" Ah !" thought Mr. Bohun, as he retraced his steps, and took a turn on the terraces, gazing round him with a sort of irrritable ecstacy, " no renovating hand can venture to renovate here ! *You* want no improving hand, beautiful old house ! I only hope she may admire, appreciate, and love you as you deserve. Inside you seem very new and strange ; but outside—outside you are still primitive and peerless, and—thank goodness— unchangeable !"

So when Mr. Bohun re-entered the hall, with its many-coloured new coir matting, and smelt the paint and the putty, and the varnish and the oil- cloth, he hurried—not to say rushed—into his own precincts, looking straight before him; nor did his own easy expression return to his face until, opening a side-door, he found himself in the only room in the house in which not a chair, nor a table, nor a carpet, curtain, shelf, nor book had been touched.

But he did not hug himself in morose solitude. On the rug lay his friend and inseparable companion, Hector, a gigantic bloodhound, who, on his master's entrance, rose like a lion from his lair, and welcomed his return by placing his fore paws with dignified gravity on his shoulders, and, with an attention intended to be complimentary, licking the face which he thus brought to a level with his own.

CHAPTER VIII.

SIR FELIX and Lady Bohun had been six weeks in Paris. In that six weeks they managed to spend two thousand pounds, what with one thing and another, and then Sir Felix began to think it was time to return home. But the bride thought the contrary. She was delighted with her life abroad, charmed with the shops, and bewildered with the power thus suddenly placed in her hands, of buying whatever she fancied, whether of furniture, dress, or *bijouterie*.

In vain, when piece after piece of tasty furniture struck her fancy and was ordered home, in vain Sir Felix represented to her that it would not suit Bohun Court, it was not the style of the house.

" Then it must be the style of my rooms," was all the answer she gave him; and he soon found it was better to be silent and submit, than to argue, for independently of doing no good, he saw an evil would arise from the opposition to her wishes, on which he had never calculated— she would take a dislike to Bohun Court—and this was too serious a matter to be lightly treated or braved.

" If these lovely things will look out of place in Bohun Court," she had one day exclaimed, " what a horrid old place it must be ! "

And Sir Felix shivered to think any one lived, bold enough to bestow such an epithet on his home.

Mr. and Mrs. Blackstone, though rich people, had been, from long habit, strict economists; and though Phemy was their only child, they had always thought it right to allowance her, and to insist on her keeping within that allowance. At the age of two-and-twenty she still received no more than her sixty pounds a year, and upon this, with occasional presents from her parents, she managed to make a very good show.

No wonder then that when she suddenly found Sir Felix expected her to spend the whole of that sum quarterly, she launched out into something very like extravagance, and sent home four new bonnets the first week of her arrival.

Even Ponsford ventured gently to expostulate,

" Don't you think, my lady, I had better have the bonnets you brought from home, done up here a little? otherwise, your ladyship will not like them after these Paris ones."

" Oh, no, Ponsford—throw them away—or stay, perhaps they will do for Bohun Court; yes —keep them for Bohun Court."

" Ladies dress a good deal about that neighbourhood in the shooting season, my lady. You will be glad of your Paris bonnets then."

" Well, pack them all up then. I can take a turn of each. How many have I?"

" Seven, my lady."

Lady Bohun reflected a moment. She was not quite sure whether Ponsford did not expect her to say, " you may have my old ones; " but she could not make up her mind to do that, so she repeated, " Pack them all up." Euphemia possessed, to use the language of a phrenologist, a bump of acquisition; and she was fond of accumulating things. For so young a girl, her love of hoarding was singular, and more singular still about her were the contradictions in her character. At the very moment that she was spending hundreds on furniture and dresses, her gloves were mended up to the very tips of her fingers, and at last attracted the attention of Sir Felix.

"My dear Euphemia, whilst you are shopping," he remarked, "let me recommend you to buy some gloves. Yours do not seem to me of the very best."

" Oh," said she, carelessly, "my gloves will do very well. Nobody sees one's gloves, and if they did, there is not one hole," and she spread out her fingers in evidence.

Sir Felix was rather shocked. He was so particular about his gloves himself that he always had them made for him, and Euphemia's, mended, and worn at the tip of every finger, made a great impression on him. He thought it must be Ponsford's fault.

" No, indeed," exclaimed his bride; " Ponsford has nothing to do with my gloves. I always mend my own. I like to do it, and mamma always made me. I have dozens of pairs upstairs, and if I trusted them to Ponsford she would give me a new pair every day. No thank you, Sir Felix. I am too good an economist for that."

And then crept into the mind of Sir Felix the recollection of the expenditure of two thousand pounds in six weeks—certainly not spent on gloves—but still spent. Yet she said she was a good economist! Well, perhaps, though she spent in some things, she saved in others, so he tried to feel satisfied, though whenever those taper fingers slid within his arm, he turned his eyes instinctively away, he was so afraid of encountering the whitened tips of the lilac gloves, and the darkened knuckles which she so emphatically affirmed was entirely the fault of his own coat!

" But we really had better be thinking of going home, my dear Euphemia," said he again, one day, " this unsettled life is very uncomfortable, and I am so anxious to show you Bohun Court."

" There will be plenty of time for that," she replied, in the gay, rather flippant manner which was not now quite so attractive to Sir Felix as it had once been; " Paris is so delightful. It is rather early in the year to go and bury oneself."

" I hope you will not look upon Bohun Court in that light, Euphemia. I should like you to be fond of your home."

" Oh, I dare say I shall; only I want to enjoy myself a little first. Do not fancy I shall not be fond of my home; I was always very fond of The Laurels."

Sir Felix pinched in his lips and said nothing. He could not quite reconcile himself to hearing Bohun Court and The Laurels named in the same breath. They certainly stood on the same earth, but that was all.

" Why are you in such a hurry to go back?" asked Lady Bohun, after having waited to see if he would make any reply.

" I am so anxious for your opinion......" began Sir Felix.

" Oh, yes, I know that," she interrupted; " but you know we *must* go some day, so I shall be sure to see it in time, only I want to know why you are in such a hurry?"

" I do not call it a hurry, my dear Euphemia. Our absence was intended to be about six weeks. It is now going on for three months."

" And such happy months! I don't know when I ever enjoyed myself so much."

This was very flattering and almost unanswerable. Still, in Sir Felix's pocket there happened to be a letter......so he returned courageously to the attack.

" I am delighted to hear it, but we may vary the scene of our happiness, I trust, Euphemia."

" Ah, Sir Felix! no shops like these at your dearly beloved Bohun Court, *I'm* sure!"

Sir Felix bit his lips. " No shops, but the beauties of nature, my dear Euphemia."

And now it was Lady Bohun's turn to bite *her*

lips. She put her head on one side and began playing with her rings.

" You had some letters to-day, Sir Felix?"

" Yes—that is, not letters, but a letter," said the matter-of-fact bridegroom.

" You never show me your letters. I thought married people always saw each other's letters?"

" My dearest......" Sir Felix instantly began turning out his pockets; " all my letters are open to you—here are half-a-dozen—can you really wish to read through such a mass of uninteresting correspondence? I wish you would always do so, and take it off my hands—here they are."

Lady Bohun was disappointed. " Oh, dear, no," she exclaimed; " I don't care for general correspondence, only you were such a time over that letter this morning."

" That was from my brother, from Guy. It is very long, but if you would like to wade through it......and such a hand as he writes......"

Lady Bohun fancied these were excuses made to prevent her seeing Mr. Bohun's letter, so she was all the more determined to have it.

" I don't mind the length," she said, " if it is all about Bohun Court, which I suppose it is?"

" Yes, and all about the farms and the stock,

which I fear you may find tedious," answered Sir Felix, searching for it.

" No, I do not think I shall. I want to know the old place well, before even I see it," said his young wife, and with these little flatteries Sir Felix was always so instantly overcome, that in another moment the letter was in her hand, and whilst he sat quietly down to his newspaper, her ladyship devoured the contents of the first epistle she had ever seen from Mr. Bohun.

Not but what she knew his handwriting well. Every day had she seen it, and every day had she determined she would summon courage to assert her right over her husband's epistolary correspondence, but till to-day the opportunity had not so easily occurred. She was a little disappointed to find that there had been no difficulty made about it. This very much deteriorated the value of the letter, but still having opened the door, she did not mean to allow it to close again, so with exemplary patience she plodded on, till she came to " your ever affectionate brother, Guy Bohun."

It was all stupid enough, but fortunately there was a postscript.

" I hope you are not going to be an absentee much longer. People are already wondering at your long stay abroad, and I have made all the excuses that I can possibly invent, so in pity to me and the neighbours, come back."

Yes—it was fortunate there was that postscript, otherwise Lady Bohun's quick blood would have had no chance of boiling up. That postscript contained exactly all she expected. It was the secret influence which had been at work all day, and had sufficed to set her wishes on one side. Sir Felix was going to obey those few lines instead of her wishes, and she clenched the thin paper in her hand with a suspicious smile upon her lips. It was quite enough that Mr. Bohun should command everything at Bohun Court, but his power should extend no further. What right had he to hope anything about the movements of Sir Felix and herself? What business had the neighbours to make remarks? What possible claim had they on her pity, that she should relinquish one hour of enjoyment for their sakes?

Not she, indeed. Before she read that letter, she had been beginning to think she had had enough of what Ponsford called "foreign parts," but now she had altered her mind. No Bohun Court for some time to come, and if Mr. Bohun and the neighbours liked to wonder or complain, why—let them.

"If Sir Felix insists on going back for the next six weeks, Ponsford," said her ladyship that evening, "I must have an attack of illness—can you manage that?"

Ponsford laughed in her gentle, respectful way.

"Oh yes, my lady, quite well."

"What shall we say or do? because you know I shall not like to shut myself up."

"Oh no, my lady. Your ladyship need not be strong enough to travel, and yet quite well enough to go about as usual."

"But I never was ill or delicate in my life, and I always have such a colour."

"I can alter the style of your hair, my lady, and if your ladyship will wear blue for a little while......"

"But I look such a fright in blue."

"Only pale, my lady, which is what will be necessary......"

"So it will! that will do famously. But suppose Sir Felix should go and leave me? Mr. Bohun may urge him so strongly......"

Lady Bohun stopped short. She knew Mr. Bohun's influence, but did not like to own it, even to herself, much less to Ponsford, who, however, was as well aware of it as if Sir Felix himself had confessed it to her.

But Ponsford had great tact. She never by word, look, or sign, betrayed the knowledge she possessed; she seemed to have the faculty of finding out everybody's weak point without their being the least aware of it; and certainly before she had lived one month with Lady Bohun, she had completely fathomed the depths of her character, and unravelled the thread of all her intricate motives.

At the idea of Sir Felix going home without his bride, even at the most urgent request of his brother, Ponsford almost laughed.

· " Oh! my lady, Mr. Bohun may be able to do a good deal with Sir Felix, but not so much as that. Of course, if your ladyship thinks the early autumn at Bohun Court would be unhealthy— and sometimes the fall of the leaf is very bad for people—why then, it would be very unwise to risk it."

Oh! wise Ponsford. This happy suggestion was a much brighter idea than the fit of illness, because it entailed no self-sacrifice; so the next time Sir Felix began upon his everlasting theme, Euphemia was ready.

" Dear Sir Felix, is Bohun Court a very woody place?"

" Oh yes, magnificently wooded," he answered

enthusiastically, " so much so, that I have often thought of thinning the timber a little, only my brother always objected."

Lady Bohun longed to say she wondered what business he had to object, only as such an observation at that moment might not have been politic, she refrained, and kept to her subject.

"Do the trees come very close up to the house, Sir Felix?"

"Yes, my dear. The Bohun woods, which are quite famous in the county, come as near to the back of the house as I am now sitting to you."

Euphemia was at that moment in one window of their apartment, and Sir Felix in the other.

"Good gracious!" she exclaimed; "but how damp that must make it."

"I never heard so," said Sir Felix; "what put that idea into your head?"

"Why common sense itself must tell one so," retorted her ladyship, with more warmth than politeness; "I remember when the leaves were falling round The Laurels, mamma always took me away."

"And why?" asked Sir Felix, innocently.

"Because it was unwholesome to remain; and besides, she thought it dangerous for me. You know I am an only child, Sir Felix. I have been used to great care."

"And that you shall always continue to have, I am sure," was her husband's reply; "but I doubt if the leaves have begun to fall yet round Bohun Court."

"But they will begin very soon. I wish you would wait another month or so, Sir Felix."

"Oh, my dear Euphemia!"

"If you do not, you will take me there just in the middle of all the damp, and you will see I shall be ill."

"I hope and trust not. The majority of the trees round our house are nice dry firs. Oh, my dear Euphemia, when I think of the delicious scent of those pine woods on a warm day, when the sun has been drawing out their rich fragrance, I quite grieve that you have missed the summer season there!"

"Never mind. Plenty of summers to come, I hope; but defend me from the autumn. I can stand a winter, Sir Felix, but mamma always used to say my chest would never bear an autumn amongst foliage."

Poor Sir Felix was sorely puzzled, and sadly vexed. In vain he brought up every argument in his power, but the lady was obdurate; that is, she said she would go, if he wished it, with pleasure. Oh yes, if he insisted, she would certainly go, but if she took cold and went into a decline, he must not mind; if it killed her, she could not help it. And after that, what could he say? what could he do? Why, submit, of course; and so the autumn sped on, and all the glorious tints of the Bohun woods faded into a dull brown, and the old house stood out gray, cold, bare, and cheerless-looking, grimly waiting to welcome as solemnly as possible, the tardy footsteps of Sir Felix and Lady Bohun.

And still they lingered, not abroad, but absent, sometimes at one gay place, and sometimes at another.

CHAPTER IX.

AND now, behold, at last they come.

The world lay under a canopy of snow. Snow covered the lawn, except where little paths had been swept out. Snow hung on the bushes, the hedges, the plants, and the buildings. It fringed the firs, and weighed down the laurels. It gave Bohun Court a white background instead of a black, and the gray stones of the house with every projection marked out in snow, looked like a drawing on a slate.

It was in such weather as this, on a bitter, damp, gusty evening, that Sir Felix and Lady Bohun drove into the court-yard, and the great bell rang, a sound which was immediately followed by the barking of many dogs, amongst which, louder than all, was heard the deep bay of a bloodhound.

"Goodness!" exclaimed Lady Bohun, in the

moment that elapsed before the carriage steps were let down, "there is a horrid dog howling. How unlucky !"

"Not howling," said Sir Felix, jumping out ; "it is only old Hector, my brother's bloodhound, and his voice is reckoned his great beauty."

Now, if I were an orthodox novelist, I should describe how the servants, drawn up in two lines in the hall, headed on one side by the house-keeper, and on the other by the butler, welcomed their new mistress as their old master led her through the admiring throng. But it was not so.

The butler had certainly been waiting some time in the hall, because the train happened to be late, but he and the footman were the only ser-vants to be seen at first, and Euphemia had walked half across the hall by herself, before she was met by Mr. Bohun, and then it was merely the usual greetings, and a hope expressed that she was hungry, and not tired, and a question as to how soon they would like dinner.

All very matter-of-fact, and very simple and homely, and Euphemia at once found herself standing by the fire in the drawing-room as if she had just returned from a drive, except that her eyes wandered restlessly round the room with curious interest, and she felt a restraint in the presence of Mr. Bohun which she could not conceal.

Then in came Sir Felix, rubbing his hands.

" What a night! How d'ye do, Guy? Rejoiced to be at home again, I assure you, but never intend to come by that train again. Stopped at every station on the line, and half an hour behind time at the last. Well, my dear Euphemia, welcome home; this is the drawing-room; rather large for comfort, but still it was as well you should be received here."

" There is a fire in the octagon for after dinner," observed Mr. Bohun, who had by this time wheeled a chair to the fire, and given Euphemia a screen and a footstool, " and my sister has now only to say how soon she would like to have it served."

Euphemia felt very strange, and very silent. She allowed Sir Felix to answer for her. Even at this first hour in her new home—her very own home—she felt annoyed to see Mr. Bohun so completely take the lead, so completely at his ease as master of the house, whilst she, and her husband, too, for the matter of that, were welcomed as though they were visitors!

But her better nature taught her that these were rebellious thoughts which must be kept down, so, though enveloping herself in a mantle of proud reserve, she forbore uttering a word. She rose from her seat, when Sir Felix said the sooner they had dinner the better, and expressed a wish for Ponsford.

"My maid," she added, as Mr. Bohun looked inquiringly at her.

"Oh!" he exclaimed, "no doubt she is in your room. Let me have the pleasure of being *cicerone* this first evening. I shall enjoy showing you through the labyrinths of passages, if I may—or would you prefer......?"

He paused, uncertain, from her manner, whether she wished it or not.

He was so open and straightforward himself, that any reserve on the part of those with whom he was associated puzzled him, and he attributed hers to shyness. Perhaps she would rather Sir Felix showed her about? Yes, that must be it, for her answer was,

"Oh! thank you, Mr. Bohun, don't trouble yourself, Sir Felix will show me the way. I need not dress to-night, only I suppose some one has taken Ponsford to my room."

"Where have I heard that name?" thought Mr. Bohun to himself, as he stood on the hearth-rug and watched his graceful sister swim out of

the room; "it seems as familiar to me as if
I had known it all my life. Where can I have
heard it?"

Meanwhile, Sir Felix drew Euphemia's arm
through his, and led her up the immense well-
staircase which, branching off at the top, led to
rooms each way by two galleries.

"This gallery to the right leads to all *our*
rooms," said Sir Felix, "and that to the left to
the visitors. This is your room, my dear Euphemia," he added, coming upon a blaze of light, a
bright fire and wax candles showing everything
off to advantage, "and my dressing-room is
exactly opposite."

"And Mr. Bohun's?" asked Euphemia, on the
impulse of the moment.

"That door at the end. Ah! my good Mrs.
Dance, I am glad to see you again! My dear
Euphemia......"

There stood Ponsford by the dressing-table, all
the glittering toilet appendages already laid out,
herself as calm and collected as though she had
been there for months instead of minutes, and by
her side a little trim old woman, curtsying nervously.

Euphemia had heard a great deal of Mrs.
Dance. Sir Felix was never weary of talking of

F 5

his old servants; but, for a wonder, his bride felt
ho jealousy of the little old housekeeper, but received her welcome as graciously as possible,
although the moment the door had closed on her,
she sank into a chair and exclaimed,

"Oh! thank goodness, Ponsford, some of the
ordeal is over at all events! Shall I have to
shake hands with the antediluvian old butler,
too? And pray tell me, is this the room the
former Lady Bohun slept in and died in? because if
it is, no power on earth shall make *me* sleep in it?"

"The last Lady Bohun was a great invalid, my
lady, and she never slept on this floor to my
knowledge. Her ladyship's apartments were all
on the ground-floor, for I have often seen Mr.
Bohun wheel her from one room to the other."

"Where was Sir Felix?" asked Euphemia.

"I don't know, my lady," was Ponsford's
quiet answer; and Lady Bohun, whilst a few
alterations were being made in her dress, fell
into deep thought.

When Ponsford had finished her arrangements,
Euphemia, still almost in a reverie, opened her
door to find her way down to the drawing-room.
The gallery was dark oak, with a strip of red
carpet running down the middle, and though
lighted at intervals by tall bronzed branches on

columns, each holding five candles, it still looked
very sombre—very different to the gay landing
of The Laurels !

But waiting in the gallery was Sir Felix, ready
again to draw her arm within his own, and take
her down to the dining-room, which he did with
a sort of proud, pleased, alacrity. She was just
on the point of making some cheerful remark on
his gallantry, when Mr. Bohun suddenly emerged
from his side door in the hall, and she froze within
herself and was silent.

Then Sir Felix led her to her own seat at the
head of what was now her own table, and, as he
did so, in words inaudible to any ear but hers, he
whispered,

" Welcome home !"

Perhaps, had there not been a third person
present, some word of thanks, some look of grati-
tude, some smile of gratified affection would have
repaid him, but as it was......no......she could not
speak before that third person......she felt the
blood rush into her face, and she caught her husband's pleased smile, for he knew by this time
that she was not a demonstrative character, and
that a blush from her was worth a volume of
words from any one else, but she could not
speak.

Fortunately, however, Sir Felix was satisfied, or perhaps he might have been too much occupied the next moment in seeing that all the table appointments were as they should be; be that as it might, he instantly began an animated conversation, and Euphemia sipped her soup and looked round.

Her first impression of everything was, "How very handsome." Her next, "But very old-fashioned."

Yes, it might be old-fashioned; but still, could even she find a fault in it?

Immediately before her was a silver soup-tureen, perfectly plain, but of a form so peculiar that it was a curiosity in itself; two quaint, oval, silver side-dishes, also of a fashion of very many days gone by; silver salt-cellars, a curious silver basket in the middle of the table, full of oranges, between every one of which was stuck a little sprig of laurestinus; and at each corner of the table a large silver candlestick. To complete all, the plates were silver, too; and to Euphemia's eyes, this was a very grand display, after the white-and-gold china which was the every-day service at The Laurels.

So she sat and looked at it all, and was pleased, for it was all hers. She wondered whether it was spread out for her especial welcome that day? Yet hardly—for everything was so quietly done— just as if it were the same every day of their lives. And then her thoughts wandered to The Laurels, and·her suburban neighbours, and she thought how much she should like Mrs. Washington to see her at the head of such a table as this.

She had plenty of time during that first dinner in her new home to indulge her thoughts, for Sir Felix and Mr. Bohun talked to each other incessantly. In vain the latter tried to draw his sister-in-law into conversation; no sooner had she replied, than Sir Felix broke in with some question or observation of his own, generally something connected with Bohun Court or its neighbourhood, or else something about his horses or dogs, and then Euphemia's chance of joining in was at at end.

She was not much flattered by this. She had not the justice to watch and see which of the brothers led the conversation into these uninteresting channels, but immediately laid all the blame upon Mr. Bohun; so to punish him, no sooner was the dessert put on the table, than, afraid of venting her displeasure in words, she leant back in her chair, and made no attempt to conceal a wide yawn.

Sir Felix, in the middle of a sentence, looked at her, and abruptly ceased speaking. Mr. Bohun, on the contrary, immediately exclaimed—

" I am sure you are very tired, and all these details must be very wearisome to you."

" I *am* tired," was her reply; " but not by your conversation; for, to tell you the truth, I have not been listening since you began upon dogs and horses."

" Then we had better adjourn," said Sir Felix, rising hastily; " and I must apologise for having been oblivious to everything except the fact that Guy and I have not met for six months. Let me show you now to the round drawing-room as we call it—it makes a warm little room for the winter evenings."

And he led the way with an alacrity which told Mr. Bohun a tale. It whispered that he did not quite know what the fair lady might say next, and so the sooner he cut short her remarks the better, since evidently something had put her out.

" But she is tired," thought her brother-in-law; " and tired people are apt to be cross. I shall see her to more advantage in the morning, so to-night all that she says and does shall go for nothing."

And it was well that he made up his mind this should be the case, for certainly during the whole of the tedious two hours after dinner, the young Lady Bohun dropped anything but pearls and diamonds from her lips, but seemed determined to keep her husband in a perpetual state of doubt and disquietude, not unmingled with dread, till he lighted her candle to retire for the night.

CHAPTER X.

THE next morning Mr. Bohun certainly saw his sister-in-law to advantage in one respect, for as he sat at breakfast he could not help thinking to himself she was the prettiest woman he had ever beheld. All he wished was, that she would always laugh, and never smile. The laugh showed a row of dazzling teeth—what the French would call a *superbe rangée*—but the smile was the most unpleasant that could be imagined. It was a sort of grin, a smile that might mean anything, according to the humour in which she happened to be. Mr. Bohun's eyes instinctively turned from it whenever they met it.

Then her dress. He knew a well-dressed woman when he saw one, and she had recollected what Ponsford had said on the subject, and was attired to perfection. She saw he had observed it, and she was pleased, for Sir Felix was one who never observed ladies dress at all, and she had often remarked to Ponsford that it was no use dressing for Sir Felix. If she wore black, white, or gray, it was all the same to him. His eyes never wandered from her face. Mr. Bohun's, on the contrary, rested flatteringly on her dress.

" My dear Euphemia," began Sir Felix, as soon as he sat down to breakfast, " Guy tells me that I have three hours' work before me in my study, what with reading up correspondences and giving audiences; so that I fear I must reluctantly depute him to have the pleasure of showing you about this morning, but in the afternoon I shall be at your service."

Lady Bohun turned her eyes towards the window. The sun shone brightly on a dazzling expanse of snow.

" I don't call this a morning for any Christian to go out, if you mean me to walk," was her answer.

" My dear, the choice of the morning's entertainment rests with yourself," continued her husband; " and as for the means of seeing the grounds, let me recommend a pony. Guy, is little Surrey in the stable still?"

Before Mr. Bohun could reply, Lady Bohun exclaimed—

" Oh ! don't ask on my account. I would as
soon ride a donkey as a pony; and far rather
walk, if I must go out."

" No must in the case, my dear ; I only thought
you would like to see the gardens and the
grounds."

" Such a day for seeing anything, dear Sir
Felix."

"Fine and seasonable, my dear Euphemia."

" I don't like seasonable weather. In Summer,
it means intensely hot; in Autumn, so damp that
you catch your death; in Spring, sharp and
showery; and in Winter, bitter like to-day."

Mr. Bohun laughed. "You are right," said
he, " it is too true. But as my brother's time is
so taken up this morning, would you let me show
you all the old family pictures in the gallery ?"

" Good gracious !" thought Euphemia to herself,
" these men think of nothing but their house and
its possessions !—Oh, thank you !" she said aloud,
" but as the sun happens to shine, and I see people
sweeping the paths, I should not mind taking a
walk for once in a way; but I tell you honestly,
Mr. Bohun, I cannot bear muddy lanes and
dripping shrubberies, and all that sort of thing.
On a cold day at The Laurels, I used only to
walk up and down the conservatory."

"Not much exercise, my dear," said Sir Felix, smiling innocently.

"Indeed!" she retorted, somewhat indignantly, "it was twenty feet long."

"Well, you can do the same here, if you like," rejoined her husband, pointing to the end of the room; "that door opens into ours."

Lady Bohun glanced carelessly round.

"Is there a conservatory there?" said she, in an indifferent voice; "I never even saw the glass doors. Is it a pretty good size?"

"Guy," exclaimed Sir Felix, slily, "how many feet long, eh?"

"Seventy," said his brother, quietly, and there was a pause.

Lady Bohun spoke very little more at breakfast; only as she was passing out of the room in answer to a question of Mr. Bohun's.

"Is it to be the seven leagued boots?" said he, with his bright, kindly smile.

"If you please," was her answer.

"What hour would suit you?"

"About twelve, I suppose, is the best time," and she sailed away without further remark.

It had been a very stiff, silent breakfast table. For the first time in his life, Mr. Bohun had felt himself a third person. There was something in

Lady Bohun's manner even on this, the very
onset of their acquaintance, which induced this
feeling. It was not fancy on his part. He felt
it for a fact, and could only hope that when she
knew him better she would like him more, and as
a natural consequence, make him feel this position less.

And full of this spirit of conciliation he lighted
his cigar and walked off to the conservatory to
benefit the plants, and to await the lady's pleasure.

The arrival of the new Lady Bohun at Bohun
Court had made a great sensation in the household; but there was another actor on the same
stage whose appearance had created an almost
equal stir, and this was Ponsford.

Ponsford, coming to Bohun Court with her
quondam mistresses as a visitor, had always been
a great lady; but coming now as Lady Bohun's
own maid, she was a greater lady still, and when
old Mrs. Dance awoke on this first morning of
her presence in the house, it was with that weight
of some undefined misfortune with which one's
steeped senses generally awake charged, if anything unusual or startling has occurred the night
before.

She and Ponsford were to breakfast together

that day, and this was the incubus, yet Ponsford
was a person of such suavity that the only wonder was, how any one could ever be afraid of her.
Yet this was certainly old Mrs. Dance's sensation. She was afraid of Ponsford's elegance,
Ponsford's calm remarks, and Ponsford's graceful
caps. Moreover, Ponsford always spoke of Lady
Bohun as "her ladyship," and this struck awe
into all the old fashioned servants' minds, for to
them, the two Ladies Bohun, under whose gentle
sway they had all lived, had never been addressed
or spoken of as anything but "my lady."

"Will my lady please to come to my room,
Mrs. Ponsford?" asked she, when their *tête-à-tête*
was over, "or shall I go up and take her orders
for dinner?"

Mrs. Ponsford said she would go and inquire,
and in half an hour she returned.

"Her ladyship begs me to tell you, Mrs.
Dance, that she will not trouble you to come up;
and as her ladyship is going out walking with
Mr. Bohun she intends resting in her room until
then; but about the dinner, provided you see
that there is fish, and something of chicken, and
something of sweetbread—these are her ladyship's own words—she does not the least care
what she has."

Mrs. Dance was silent from perplexity. At last she said—

"My lady no doubt means she would wish me to draw up a bill of fare."

"Not at all, Mrs. Dance, I assure you. To tell you a little secret, her ladyship cannot bear anything like trouble, and she is not the least particular about her dinner; indeed, I always ordered it for her when we were abroad. I am certain she will be quite satisfied with your selection, provided, of course, you recollect that her ladyship makes a point of fish, and chicken, and sweetbreads."

Poor Mrs. Dance was still sorely puzzled. This was not at all what she had expected, nor anything like what she had ever been accustomed to. The ordering of dinner had always been quite an important ceremony at Bohun Court in the lifetime of the former Ladies Bohun, and even after their death, Mrs. Dance had been in the habit of attiring herself especially for this ceremony in an appropriate costume, and waiting on Mr. Bohun in the library to take his orders. Had she lived to take orders, and such indefinite orders, too, from the lady's maid?

No. But the old woman was meek and very

gentle, so instead of exploding, she thought she would merely try again.

"Chickens, of course, my lady can have whenever she pleases, but I fear, Mrs. Ponsford, unless the coach is ordered to leave fish regularly at the gate, we shall have some difficulty just at first. Mr. Bohun had fish just when the man in the village happened to have any over, but it is so out of the way here, that we have to write a general order when our dinners begin, and Mr. Bohun said I was to ask my lady, when I applied to him."

"Of course," said Ponsford, slightly rearing her head in a manner peculiar to herself; "of course her ladyship orders everything now; but fish she must have, that I know. It must be arranged somehow."

"I will send directly," said Mrs. Dance, "but perhaps my lady will allow me to see her, to take her commands for the future."

"*I* dare not disturb her ladyship, *you* may, if you like to venture," returned the lady's maid.

"I mean about the sweetbreads," persisted Mrs. Dance, quite distressed; "there can be none to-day, I much fear, for they only kill veal once a week, Mrs. Ponsford, and the day is past. We shall always have to bespeak whilst the neighbourhood is so full."

"You do not intend to say that her ladyship actually cannot have sweetbreads when she pleases?" exclaimed Ponsford.

"They only kill once a week," persisted the housekeeper.

"Then my good Mrs. Dance," retorted her companion, impressively, preparing to swim out of the room with equal grace and dignity; "they must kill a calf on purpose, that's all I have to remark."

Whereupon she left Mrs. Dance to her perplexity and distress, and rejoined her mistress, who was unpacking her Parisian *bijouterie*, and brushing it with a tiny jeweller's brush dipped in eau de Cologne.

"Have you got me out of it, Ponsford?"

"Yes, my lady. I said you could not possibly be disturbed."

"What will she do to-morrow, do you think? Plague me again with her clean apron and curtsies?"

"Oh, no, my lady. I can arrange it again to-morrow till she becomes accustomed to my ordering dinner, and then your ladyship will have no further trouble."

But Ponsford, clever and useful as she was, did not quite understand Mrs. Dance. The old lady was not going to be silenced without a remonstrance. She did not intend, meek as she was, to resign her prerogative without a struggle, so straightway she sought Mr. Bohun (not Sir Felix—Sir Felix was nobody in comparison), and found him smoking in the conservatory.

It took her very few minutes to detail her grievance, and to her infinite relief and consolation, Mr. Bohun entered into it immediately.

"It was my fault, Mrs. Dance; nobody's fault but mine. Sir Felix, you know, never thinks of these things, so all the arrangements ought to have been cut and dried by me, and placed before Lady Bohun in proper form. She would then have known that it was the custom of the house for you to wait on her every morning for her commands. Dear old Dance, don't fret. It shall all be right to-morrow."

"But, sir, I fear not. If it were only my lady I had to deal with, I might hope, but it is that fine maid. Then about the fish......"

"There again my fault! How could I have been so stupid as never to tell Horsman to begin sending it again every day? All my selfishness, not caring for fish myself, and also, perhaps, their

arrival having been so often fixed and then put
off again, and then so unexpected at the last.
However, never mind Goody Dance."

" Ah, sir, but my lady may mind very much."

"Not she. She is young, and gay, and pretty,
and may care for silks and satins, but not so very
much for good dinners."

" My lady's maid, sir, made such a point of the
sweetbreads, that I think my lady *does* mind what
she has, but as for them, why, that's an impossi-
bility, sir."

" Then of course you said so?"

" Yes, sir, I did."

" And what did this grand lady's maid say?"

" Why, sir, she said, as composed and cool as
I am now, and more, 'then,' says she, 'you must
kill a calf on purpose.'"

Mr. Bohun could now preserve his gravity no
longer, but at this climax burst into a fit of un-
controllable laughter.

" The best thing I ever heard in my life!" he
exclaimed; "I should like to see the individual
who made the remark. But now take my advice,
Mrs. Dance. Wait till I have seen and spoken
to Lady Bohun. I am going to walk with her
this morning, and I dare say I shall have an opportunity of setting things right. If not, Sir Felix

will. Any way, do not let a new maid put out our dear old Dance, so trot along and send up as good a dinner to-day as you did yesterday, and all will be well in the end."

So he thought. But he had not until now come into contact with any one resembling the new Lady Bohun. He was "reckoning without his host," as the saying is.

In a few minutes more she joined him in the conservatory, and as she made her way cautiously between the plants, ejaculations fell from her lips at every step.

"Ugh! ach!" and sundry others. "One can see that it is some time since you entertained a lady at Bohun Court, Mr. Bohun. If I have a horror of anything, it is smoke—cigars, I mean; I never suffer Sir Felix to smoke. If you will allow me, I will put off my inspection of the conservatory until it is purified a little. I did not know you were smoking."

Mr. Bohun hastily threw away the offender, with many apologies. "He had no idea she would have been ready so soon," he said. "He did not know that his brother had given up this vice—he fancied Lady Bohun would by this time have been quite inured to it. But, since you dislike it, I shall make a point of abstaining for the future," he added, and Euphemia bent her head in token of acceptance of the apology.

They then started on their walk, and as he followed in the wake of a black moiré antique of fabulous dimensions, Mr. Bohun had time to examine and make mental comments on his new sister. He regarded her rather as a curiosity, and certainly her dress for that country walk in the depth of winter, was young female England to perfection.

She had on, as I before said, a dress of black moiré antique. It was looped up all round over a red petticoat of quilted silk. A tight black cloth jacket profusely braided, a wide-awake with a red feather, and turn-down collars with a red ribbon under them, completed the upper part of her attire. But it was on her feet that the eyes of Mr. Bohun rested in profound surprise. She had boots, the heels of which reminded him of nothing so forcibly as the favourite chaussure of Mother Shipton—high pointed heels, laced with red.

"I should like," thought he to himself, as he gazed, "to show her to Mrs. Traut." And then he thought better of it. "No, not in this guise. The impression would be startling and ineffaceable. I could not present, in a costume like this, the new Lady Bohun."

So she had actually at last become Lady Bohun in his sight? Yes—he who had thought he never could look at her except as Miss Blackstone, now saw in her a Lady Bohun so completely standing alone in her own fashion, that she sent the memory of her predecessors back into the abyss of the past, and was too utterly unlike either to provoke even the faintest comparison.

CHAPTER XI.

Mr. Bohun had come out to escort his sister
over the grounds, to show her the gardens, and
conduct her through the leafless shrubberies. Did
she permit him to do so? Not she. The paths
had all been swept a certain width, over which
her draperies extended on both sides at least a
foot; thus, to attempt to walk by her side was
impossible. So he had to follow her, and as she
walked very fast, never asked him the way, but
pursued whichever path she pleased, talking incessantly to him in a voice which rang loud and
clear in the frosty air, and never once turning her
head to see where he was, he felt very much as if
the tables were turned, and *he* was the one to be
shown the way..

On, and on, and on they went; in and out of
the small iron gates, up and down the acclivities

and declivities, the lady still taking the lead, till at last she stopped from sheer want of breath.

"Well, Mr. Bohun," she panted, "I hope you are satisfied now. I am sure I have walked far and fast enough to please anybody, but I tell you honestly I am not going to be taken much further. Are there no benches, or arbours, or any resting-places anywhere?" And her eyes glanced restlessly round.

She looked very beautiful, eyes sparkling, and cheeks glowing, otherwise he longed to say something severe upon the dance she had led him, but unfortunately a pretty woman may go a long way with an impunity denied to an ugly one, so he rather coldly replied that she had wandered some distance from the grounds; they were now on the confines of the Bohun woods.

"Oh, Mr. Bohun, why in the world then did you come so far? How am I to get back again?"

Still preserving his equanimity, he informed her that the only mode by which she could return was that by which she came. If she pleased to vary the route, he would be happy to show her another way.

"A shorter cut?" she asked.

"No—much about the same distance, only through the woods instead of the open ground."

"And get wet through? no, thank you, Mr. Bohun. Then I will go back the way we came, though perhaps I may drop with fatigue by the way. However, that will not be *my* fault," and the emphasis was not flattering.

Mr. Bohun then bethought him of Mrs. Trant's cottage. It stood just midway between where they now paused, and Bohun Court, and though Lady Bohun was neither in a humour nor a costume to render her a desirable companion to introduce just at that moment, still it was better than permitting her to over-fatigue herself, and be blamed for it by Sir Felix, for though his brother had hardly been at home four-and-twenty hours, Mr. Bohun had discovered that the lady possessed considerably the upper hand, and had begun to try and mould him to her every will and whim. So, very hesitatingly, he suggested that there was a cottage at no great distance, where, if she liked, she might rest.

"Mamma never let me go into cottages. She was so afraid of infectious disorders," was Lady Bohun's answer.

"Oh, but there are no children in the cottage I mean. It belongs to an old lady—a dear old retainer, if I may so call her—one of whom you may probably have heard from my brother—Mrs. Trant."

"Do you mean the old governess?" asked Lady Bohun.

The question was abrupt, and it jarred on Mr. Bohun's nerves. It was the second time that day that she had given him a similar twinge, and he could not help feeling that there was a want of good taste both in the tone with which she had uttered the words, "the old governess?" as well as in the sentence with which she had greeted him in the conservatory, namely, "one can see that it is some time since you entertained a lady at Bohun Court!"

These words had struck him as wanting in good feeling, and the former in good taste. Mr. Bohun was gifted with no small amount of penetration. He was beginning to see that his fair sister was something more than a spoilt child, but he answered calmly,

"Yes, the same. She was my mother's governess, and remains one of our most attached friends; but, Lady Bohun," (he had such a dislike to the name of Euphemia, that he felt he could never use it, and so began at once to call her Lady Bohun), "she is very old, and not very strong......I am not quite sure but what I ought

G 5

to prepare her for your visit, if you are kind
enough to call on her......"

" But is there anywhere else to rest?"

" No, not for two miles."

" Then call I must, whether I like it or not,
for rest I must have.   Now, Mr. Bohun, lead the
way, if you please, and don't take me twenty
miles round."

So off they started again, the lady silent
because through the woods there were no paths
swept, and she was obliged to be careful, and the
gentleman silent, devising how he.could possibly
dissuade her from paying this visit.

When quite at his wit's end, she suddenly
rescued him from despair.

" Mr. Bohun, I feel that if I once sit down in
a chair you will never get me up again.   I had
better not call on your old lady to-day, so just
walk on, and if it is the proper thing for me to
pay the visit, I can come with Sir Felix another
day."

And with this they rapidly pursued the wind-
ing paths till they came out at the back of Bohun
Court, and found themselves in the ivy-grown
quadrangle round which were ranged the dog-
kennels.

No sooner did Mr. Bohun appear, than every

tenant started out of his retirement, with a yell
of joy, and Lady Bohun held her hands up to her
ears in pretended agony. Amidst the many-
toned voices, rose the deep bay of Mr. Bohun's
bloodhound.

" Ah ! ah !" cried Lady Bohun, "there is *my*
enemy ! I knew him by his voice. He howled
me a welcome last night, and not satisfied with
that, kept me awake till this morning."

" You don't mean that?" said Mr. Bohun,
turning quickly towards her.

" Yes, I do. I said to Sir Felix this morning,
the first thing, if that dog were mine he should
be shot."

And now a deep colour rushed into Mr. Bohun's
face. His eyes gave a flash like fire, and biting
his lip, he turned on his heel, and left her to find
her way into the house alone.

On the stone steps he sat down and gave a
low whistle. In an instant a huge animal started
from his kennel, came bounding towards him,
and, placing his large paws on his master's
shoulders, began whining and licking his face all
over in an ecstacy of joy, whilst his bright intelli-
gent eyes sparkled with genuine happiness.

It was the hour that Hector and his master
always went into luncheon together; for seven

years this had been their invariable custom, and
never, till this day, had Mr. Bohun hesitated
about it.   To-day, however, two or three words
from careless lips, made him pause and think,
whilst the dog, seemingly surprised at the delay,
all but asked, " Why don't we go ?"

But she had called him her enemy, and said,
if it had been *her* dog...... No, Mr. Bohun could
not repeat that sentence even to himself.   He
could not imagine how anyone, after seeing the
no..... .....eature, could have the heart not to
.. .t......the noise he might make, for the sake of
his beauty.   And could anyone call that sonorous
voice a howl?   Had she not clearly said he
howled?

What would she say if they walked in to
luncheon side by side ?

" We can but try it, at all events," said he to
himself, after a few moments reflection; and
rising, they entered the house together.

Luncheon had been waiting some time.   Sir
Felix, who was the soul of punctuality, had
worried himself into a fever.   First he thought
they must have lost their way, but then that,
with his brother for pioneer, could hardly be
possible. .Then he fancied his Euphemia had
walked too far, would sit down on a snowy bank,

and catch her death of cold. Lastly, that they had gone in to see old Mrs. Trant, and this was a consolatory supposition.

But when Mr. Bohun and Hector appeared alone, his fears broke forth.

"What *has* become of Euphemia?"

Mr. Bohun, whom nothing scarcely ever agitated, hurried, or discomposed, detailed the proceedings of the morning with brief simplicity, but before he had ceased speaking, the folding doors, from the intermediate drawing-room, were thrown open, and Lady Bohun appeared. She looked annoyed.

"Not my fault, Sir Felix—if anyone is to blame it is not I. Ponsford tells me the whole house is in a state of alarm because luncheon has been on the table about ten minutes; but in the first place I had not the most remote suspicion we were tied to minutes so very strictly in this house, and in the next, if I am late, it is not my fault."

All this was uttered with a rapidity which compelled Sir Felix to wait patiently for an opening, of which he took the earliest advantage.

"My dearest, Ponsford is mistaken......"

"Dear Sir Felix, pardon me, Ponsford is never

mistaken. She knows the ways of this house better than I do, I have no doubt."

Mr. Bohun gave one of his quick upward glances, and Sir Felix turned pale, but he proceeded temperately notwithstanding.

"My dearest, I meant that the hours at Bohun Court are, of course, under your entire control, but as to a state of alarm, it is I only who have suffered......"

"Dear Sir Felix! how can you?"

"My dearest, I really imagined some catastrophe had kept you out all these hours."

"Not my fault, Sir Felix. Ask Mr. Bohun, *he* knows."

Mr. Bohun was breaking up biscuit for his dog, and a curl, half a smile, came to the corner of his lip, as he replied to the appeal by saying, "We certainly did walk much farther than we intended," and he said no more; for just then he was again puzzling himself to think where he had heard that familiar name of Ponsford.

"But since you are here, safe, sound, and blooming," continued Sir Felix, "take something to restore your exhausted energies. My dear Euphemia, chicken or some cutlets?"

Lady Bohun did not immediately answer. She had caught sight of the dog, and her eyes were fixed on it with an expression of mingled haughtiness and displeasure.

"May I ask," she began, addressing her brother-in-law, "if that dog is always your companion at meals?"

"Hitherto he has been so," said Mr. Bohun, caressing the great ears affectionately; "but if he offends in any way......"

"I cannot endure dogs—and that one, begging your pardon, Mr. Bohun, is such a monster."

"He certainly is unusually large," returned Mr. Bohun, taking the word in its least objectionable signification; "but he is as gentle as a lady's lap-dog. However, if you object, Lady Bohun......"

"Oh, never mind to-day. I don't want to create any more confusion *to-day*," she said, with marked emphasis; "only, as I don't like dogs, it is not so very pleasant."

"He shall go," said Mr. Bohun, rising.

"No, no; I beg not. Pray sit still and let us have our luncheon. Chicken, if you please, Sir Felix—only, as I said before, I hope it will be only for *to-day*."

And the luncheon went on in silence.

CHAPTER XII.

"Ponsford," said Lady Bohun, as her maid attended at her toilet that night, " I have done two great deeds to-day."

" Have you, my lady? " said Ponsford, smiling.

" Yes ; and I assure you it requires no small courage to eradicate the bad habits of a house that has been for so many years under the government of a couple of bachelors, as one may almost say."

" Very true, my lady."

" But, luckily, I am not wanting in that sort of courage, Ponsford."

" No, my lady; and it is very fortunate your ladyship is not. Many a young lady would take things just as they find them, and then no wonder many a house is made so uncomfortable."

" Quite right, Ponsford. But you will never guess how bold I have been; only fortunately I remembered what mamma's friend, Mrs. Washington, used to say, always take the bull by the horns at once; and so, when I found Mr. Bohun smoking in the conservatory—*my* conservatory— I very quickly gave him to understand that that would never do!"

"Dear me, my lady! was Mr. Bohun really guilty of such a thing? and your ladyship in the very house! But I remember people always said the last Lady Bohun quite spoiled him."

"Then I am sure *I* shall not, and I flatter myself I shall not find him smoking there again in a hurry. Well, that was one great deed, and the next was about that abominable dog of his."

"Oh, my lady! I spoke to Mrs. Dance about that, and said how it had disturbed your ladyship's rest last night, and that really I thought the dog had better be sent down to the kennels."

"Where are the kennels, Ponsford?"

"In the woods, my lady."

"Then there it shall go. But what did Mrs. Dance say?"

"Oh, my lady! she took me up quite sharply, and said I had better speak to Mr. Bohun about it, and see what his answer would be, insinuating that I might as well expect to move Bohun Court, as Hector."

"Did she really? Very well; we shall see,
then, who has most power here. But at all
events, I have put a stop to its being brought
into the room at luncheon; that I *would not*
permit."

"I should think not, my lady. But it seems to
me that Mr. Bohun has lived here so long as
master, that perhaps he hardly knows......"

"What he does not know, Ponsford, I shall be
very happy to teach," retorted the new Lady
Bohun, and with that laudable resolution, her
eyelids closed in sleep.

So had passed the first day of the new reign;
not auspiciously, thought all parties concerned.
As for Mr. Bohun, it was an era in his life, and
he could not sufficiently express his astonishment
at the singularity of this young creature's character. He could not conceal from himself that
even this slight beginning augured ill for the
future; and when he came to think over the
events of the day—a day that had seemed interminable—he recollected his promise to old Mrs.
Dance to set all things right before the next
morning, in *her* department, and now, what had
he done?—nothing! He had not had an opportunity of approaching the subject, and even if he

had, he doubted whether his moral courage would
have permitted him to enter upon it.

Such had been the effect of that day upon him,
and sleep overtook him as he still lay wondering
what the next might bring forth, and hoping
better things.

But before the arrival of that blissful tranquillity for which he was so sanguine, there was
a little affair to be settled between Mrs. Dance
and Ponsford, the rival queens.

The next morning, determined not to be extin-
guished without a struggle, Mrs. Dance prepared
as usual to wait upon " my lady " after breakfast,
to take her commands as to the various arrangements for the day; but no sooner had she set
foot on the stairs leading up to " my lady's "
room, than, as she secretly expected, she was met
by the lady's maid.

" Oh ! Mrs. Dance, her ladyship thought you
would wish to see her about this time, so I was
just coming to save you the stairs.   I am sorry to
say her ladyship is very much fatigued to-day—
quite knocked up from having over-walked herself
with Mr. Bohun yesterday."

" I am sorry to hear it, Mrs. Ponsford," replied
the old lady, drily.   " Will you please to ask my
lady if she would be so good as to give me her

orders now ? or would a later hour suit her ladyship better ?"

"I have this moment left her ladyship, Mrs.
Dance, and am authorised to say she does not feel
able to exert herself to-day, or rather this morning.
I hope she may rally a little after luncheon. Her
ladyship cares so little what she has for dinner,
that provided you are good enough to see that
there is, in addition, of course, to the fish, a *vol-
au-vent* of something tender......"

But Mrs. Dance was now upon her guard and
upon her dignity. She was nerved up to act
with the spirit which she considered necessary,
and, without a moment's hesitation, cut short
what she looked upon as the cool effrontery of her
rival.

"I thank you, Mrs. Ponsford," said she, drawing
up her prim little figure and making a stately little
curtsy; "I thank you, but pray do not trouble
yourself to give me orders ; " and, turning round,
she straightway descended to the library, where,
deep in heaps of accumulated accounts, sat Sir
Felix and Mr. Bohun.

"Sir Felix," began the old lady, addressing her
words to her master, but her looks to Mr. Bohun,
as though from him only did she expect the real
support and assistance, "I am truly sorry, Sir

Felix, to intrude on you on such a point as a difference in the household, but I have lived here, Sir Felix, fifty-five years, and never did so before, so I beg your pardon humbly. But if you please, Sir Felix, I wish to tell you, and Mr. Bohun, and my lady, as respectfully as possible, that I cannot, unless by your express orders—and even then, Mr. Bohun, I don't really think I can—I cannot take orders in this house from Mrs. Ponsford."

It was out. The fair, but faded and shrivelled cheeks, of the little old woman bore a pink spot of agitation, and her eyes twinkled, not tearfully, but with dry anger—as much anger as such pale blue eyes could show.

Sir Felix leant back in his chair, and put his hands in his pockets. Mr. Bohun looked down, and drew pictures on the blotting paper before him. Neither spoke, and then the old housekeeper proceeded to narrate her grievance, and ask for a remedy. She did not wish to intrude on my lady—she would not trouble her for the world—but she had considered it proper and respectful to see if she would like to take the complete rule of the house and the ordering of the dinners, before she took upon herself to follow the old plan of doing it all on her own responsibility.

"You know, Sir Felix—and Mr. Bohun, you

know—that I am capable of conducting this establishment, and am ready and willing to save my lady all the trouble I can; but not knowing what my lady might have been used to at her own home, I thought, perhaps, she might think it an undue liberty if I did not step up every morning, as usual, just to ascertain her wishes, and so I began at once ; but each day I have been met by Mrs. Ponsford, and stopped, and had orders given me; and this, sir, begging your pardon, I cannot put up with again, for if you remember, Mr. Bohun, I spoke to you about it yesterday, sir."

Sir Felix looked at his brother, his countenance full of vexation, and then Mr. Bohun felt he must speak.

" So you did, dear old Dance, and I am only sorry that I had no opportunity of saying a word on the subject. I am certain that to wound your feelings would be the very last thing Lady Bohun would wish to do."

" The very last thing," said Sir Felix.

" So that I have no doubt that a few words of explanation will, as I said yesterday, soon set matters right; and if you will let my brother and myself talk it over a little, and come again in half an hour, I think you will not have cause to complain again. What do you say, Felix ? "

" Quite so—I agree with you—yes, my good Dance, suppose you let Mr. Bohun talk it over with me, and come again, eh?"

" As you please, Sir Felix," said the old woman, and retired in silence.

The brothers then looked at each other.

" This is very disagreeable, Guy," said Sir Felix.

" Very," returned Mr. Bohun. " It is what most people have happening in their houses every day—a domestic row on a small scale; and some people enjoy it, but I cannot say I do."

" But what are we to do?"

" Confer with your wife, Felix. There is nothing else to be done. Depend upon it, young and inexperienced as she is, she is not aware that old servants stand a good deal upon punctilio; but if you represent things in their true light, she will see how very little will settle affairs quietly."

Sir Felix mused. " I think it is rather foolish though of Dance," said he; " she might as well have let matters take their course till we were a little settled."

" I don't think that," said Mr. Bohun; " she is an old woman of some experience, and depend upon it, she would not have spoken had she not seen the necessity. It is rather hard for an old

servant like herself to be under the orders of a
lady's maid, probably younger and more inexperienced even than......"

" Ponsford is not so very young, Guy, and by
no means inexperienced; on the contrary, she is
quite a confidential sort of person."

" Really. I have never seen her, but somehow
her name seems very familiar. Then I conclude
she was an old servant of Mrs. Blackstone's?"

" Oh, no! She only came to us when we
married. But now, Guy, do suggest something.
How are we to arrange this?"

" Speak to Lady Bohun. Request her to see
Mrs. Dance every morning for five minutes, and
give her own orders. If she dislikes this, ask her
to delegate the power to you."

" Or to you?"

" Oh, no; not to me! I am nobody here,
Felix; and I had rather not be brought into the
field at all."

" But suppose Euphemia were to wish it?"

" I do not think she will," said Mr. Bohun.

Sir Felix rose with a heavy sigh. He was
placed for the first time in his life in, to him, a
very difficult and disagreeable position. He was
about to undertake a most distasteful errand; and
he would not have confessed, even to his brother,

how doubtful he felt as to the reception his request would meet. But there was no help for it. He must go, for anything was better than hot water in the house, and so he rose to depart.

Just as he was moving towards the door, there came two or three little raps at it.

"Come in," said Sir Felix, stopping short.

The door opened and a figure entered. It was Ponsford. She did not appear to see Mr. Bohun. Her eyes were on Sir Felix; but had she looked round the room, she would probably have been rather flattered, than otherwise, to have seen the expression of dismay with which the former gazed on her, or to have heard the words which were absolutely trembling on his lips.

"The vampire, by Jove!"

"If you please, Sir Felix," said that softest of voices, "her ladyship would be very glad to speak to you for a few minutes."

The words were uttered in a gently interrogative tone, but to the ear of Sir Felix they implied a summons which demanded his immediate attention, and, moreover, obtained it; so much so, that as he left the room, Mr. Bohun ejaculated to himself, "1 wish him joy."

He was absent more than an hour; Mr. Bohun, meanwhile, feeling very much as that friend feels

who has accompanied a victim to the dentist's.
and awaits, in the ante-room, his return from the
room of torture.

And when he did return, those brothers knew
each other's faces so well, that Mr. Bohun had
but to give one glance to read at once the result
of the interview, for "defeat" was plainly written
on the brow of Sir Felix.

"I hope," began his brother, pacifically, "that
everything is pleasantly arranged."

"I found Euphemia extremely displeased," was
Sir Felix's reply.

"And why?" asked Mr. Bohun.

"Of course!" retorted the husband of half a
year, "and no wonder. I really am surprised at
old Dance; she should have known better. I
find she never even waited to hear the end of
Ponsford's sentence, but turned short round,
and came off to me. She should have waited
patiently, and made a proper request to see
Euphemia."

"Whose version of the story is this?"

"Euphemia has this moment told me."

"And did Ponsford tell her?"

"Of course."

"Is Ponsford quite and entirely to be relied on?"

"Guy?"

"Yes, I ask; because that very soft-spoken individual is not entirely unknown to me. Do you remember the vampire?"

"Pshaw, Guy! how absurd to rake up that old name. Pray do not utter it before my wife."

"Not I. But you remember her of old, do you not? Do you remember the dread with which all our servants looked forward to a visit from the Tophams, because it entailed Mrs. Ponsford? How well I seem now to know the name! Do you remember the so-called legacy of pearls left to her by Lady Mary, and the tremendous uproar it created in the family? Do you remember a certain story, carefully hushed up, of a pen held in the hand of the dying Lady Merivale?"

"Guy, you put me out of patience!" cried Sir Felix; "why revive these useless stories?"

"To put you on your guard against one who may otherwise bring dissension into our peaceful home. Don't let the vam......I mean, don't let Mrs. Ponsford set you against dear old Dance. And now to business—have you arranged matters?"

"Yes, but with some difficulty. At first Euphemia was very anxious that Ponsford should be a sort of half-and-half housekeeper, just to order dinner, or hardly that, but to say what

Euphemia wishes to have and all that; but this I thought unadvisable. Was I right?"

"And then?" said Mr. Bohun, evasively.

"Then I suggested that she should merely go through a form of seeing a bill of fare, or a list of company, and all that sort of thing; but Euphemia says that she cannot bear being tied to that kind of ceremony: very naturally, poor young thing! she has never been used even to *think* for herself, much less to manage a large establishment."

Mr. Bohun wished to remark that it might be as well, then, if she now began to learn, but he refrained, and listened patiently to Sir Felix, as he continued.

"So it ended by my asking her if she would like Mrs. Dance to take the whole into her own hands for a time, and reign sole housekeeper; and then Euphemia will be able to judge if all is conducted as she wishes, and either to alter, approve, .or find fault, as the case may be; and thus you see there will be no more disagreeables, eh, Guy?"

"A compromise," said Mr. Bohun; "yes, a very fair compromise, and I hope it may last."

"What—have you any doubts?"

"It depends."

"On what?"

"On whether the......whether Ponsford interferes or not. If she should, Dance will throw down the sceptre."

" Well, we can but try. Euphemia likes Ponsford; she is very useful to her. I should be very sorry to be the cause of her leaving."

" No fear of that," said Mr. Bohun.

" Ah, Guy ! you are very unjust to that poor woman," returned Sir Felix.

" I hope I am," was Mr. Bohun's reply, and there the dialogue ended; but his thoughts ran in the same channel for several hours afterwards, and the feeling uppermost in his mind was,

" I have heard that there is a skeleton in every cupboard. I thought Bohun Court an exception, but I suspect it has got in, even here, at last !"

CHAPTER XIII.

BOHUN COURT was full of company; four or five married couples and a daughter or two staying in the house, and people from the neighbouring country seats coming to dinner every day. It reminded the residents in the county of the old days of the first Lady Bohun, who used to come down for a few months in October with all her London-season dresses, a little crushed and a little faded, and show off to a house full of company till after Christmas.

The third Lady Bohun had now been married some six months or so, and was becoming accustomed to her new position. She was completely in her element. She ruled her husband, for he gave way to her implicitly; she ruled her household through Mrs. Dance, who gave her no trouble at all; and she ruled the fashions round Bohun Court, for she was dressed by Ponsford, and could have stood the scrutiny of a dozen French milliners.

Lady Bohun was in the ascendant; Sir Felix sunned himself humbly in her radiance, and Mr. Bohun calmly fell into the background, with a quiet dignity that won him infinite admiration. He and his sister-in-law rarely clashed; some people said it was because they mutually avoided each other, and others that it was owing to his faultless temper. Yet there were well-meaning friends and admirers of his who, in their mistaken zeal, often drew from Lady Bohun's rosy lips some of those cutting and mischievous remarks for which she had already gained herself quite a name.

There was one young lady, the only daughter of a retired old Admiral near Bohun Court, with whom Lady Bohun had this first winter formed a violent intimacy. Sir Felix had a great dislike to female friends. It was one of his opinions that a married woman should have no bosom friends, seeing that a married woman should have no secrets or confidences except with her husband, and so fully aware of this was Lady Bohun, that she had not as yet ventured to ask him to allow her to invite even her friend Fanny Washington to stay with her.

But the intimacy with Miss Maynard had been dashed into very suddenly. She had arrived one day with the Admiral, her father, to dine and sleep at Bohun Court, and having been snowed up for three days, left the house Euphemia's bosom friend.

Miss Maynard was what the world calls a very fast young lady. She was the first specimen of the kind that Lady Bohun had ever seen, and it amused her exceedingly. Motherless, and brought up entirely under her father's eye, she had received a masculine education, and had no feminine tastes.

"I cannot think how I ever came to have a daughter," the old Admiral used often to shout, at the top of his voice; "I never wanted one. I wanted a son, but I've made her as like a boy as I could," and this he evidently considered a circumstance to boast of, so that Jem, as she was familiarly called (having been christened Jemima), never stood a chance of being polished to the brilliancy of other young ladies.

The morning after the arrival of the Maynards on the occasion of this their first visit, Lady Bohun's eyes opened in dismay on the snow. The house was full of company—how could she amuse them all day?

"Ponsford, the gentlemen are sure to go out; but what on earth am I to do with the ladies?"

"Oh! my lady, you will find Miss Maynard a great assistance. I used to hear Lady Mary say, she was as good as a play, and to hear her and Mr. Bohun go on, was almost enough, with nothing else."

"Why? Does he not like her?"

"I don't know, my lady. Nobody ever knows who Mr. Bohun likes or dislikes......"

"Very true, Ponsford; I never met such a close, reserved man in my life. But do you mean, on the contrary, that there is a flirtation between them?"

"Oh! dear no, my lady. I can hardly explain; but your ladyship will soon see what I mean— nothing like a flirtation—but, somehow, Miss Maynard seemed always after Mr. Bohun, teazing him, and trying to annoy him."

"Then, if she succeeded, Ponsford, she must have some wit about her, for I never saw such an imperturbable character as he is, in all my existence. I can only say *I* never managed to annoy him."

Ponsford said nothing, but there was something peculiar in the expression of her face which caught Lady Bohun's eye.

" Ponsford, you look mysterious; do you mean to say......"

" Oh ! my lady, I never pay attention to what people say—I mean to ill-natured remarks, and all that. I was only thinking just then how very easily, in reality, Mr. Bohun *can* be annoyed."

" Can he? How do you know? About what has he ever been annoyed that you know of?"

" His dog, my lady. I am sure I thought I never should hear the last of that; and yet what lady could ever suffer such a monster as that to be made a drawing-room pet ?"

" Oh ! *that* annoyed him, did it? Serve him right, Ponsford. Besides, mamma's friend, Mrs. Washington, used always to say to all her young married daughters, if there is anything you don't like in your homes, strike at once, never hide a skeleton in your cupboards: so, you see, I spoke out at once. And about the smoking, too; I suppose that annoyed his high-mightiness as well! Did you ever hear anything of that ?"

" Never, my lady; but Mr. Bohun smokes all the same, only in his own sitting-room, which is just under my room."

" And you have the benefit of it, then ?"

" Oh ! my lady, that does not signify," said

Ponsford, with a martyr's smile, " I shut my window, that's all."

So Lady Bohun went down to breakfast, secretly satisfied that, at all events, in two instances during her reign, her power had not only been exercised, but *felt*.

Miss Maynard was already in the breakfast-room when Lady Bohun entered. She was seated up upon the corner of the side table, just behind her father, who was reading the newspaper. Mr. Bohun leant against the window opposite to them, opening letters.

" Where's Jem?" roared the Admiral, as Lady Bohun approached.

" Up here, sir."

" Get down, then. Don't you see Lady Bohun ?"

" I'm not blind, father dear, and Lady Bohun isn't deaf," said the young lady, and sprang nimbly to the ground.

Lady Bohun shot a rapid glance at Mr. Bohun, met his eyes, and saw them instantly fall again. He seemed to have been watching the effect of this new guest's appearance on her, but as yet her only feeling was extreme surprise; she neither liked her, nor disliked her, but watched her as a curiosity.

The guests gathered, one by one, round the breakfast-table, and Miss Maynard seated herself next to Mr. Bohun.

"I always make a push to be next to you, don't I, Mr. Bohun?"

"Yes, Miss Maynard, you certainly do, and it will not, I trust, make me over-value my humble powers of entertainment."

"I don't think so, since I generally find I have to amuse *you*. Now, tell me, how have you been getting on since I left you? and where is your shadow?"

"Which question am I to answer first; and who is the shadow?"

"Hector, to be sure."

"Hector, thank you, is quite well."

"And how have you fared under the new *régime?* or, as papa would say, the new flag?"

"I think I sail under very fair colours, Miss Maynard."

"Oh! yes, I know you do in one sense; she is very pretty; but, you know, I don't mean that exactly; I want to know if you get on well together? People say you don't."

Mr. Bohun was accustomed to the *brusquerie* of Miss Maynard, but even he was startled by this emphatic sentence. She perceived it, and immediately added, "You look guilty, so don't puzzle yourself to find evasions. Let us pass on, or rather go back to my opening question about Hector. I am so used to feeding him at every meal in this house, that I wish to hear the rights of it. How has he offended?"

"He has not done so, to my knowledge."

"Then why is he not here?"

"Because he is in his kennel."

"Very well, Mr. Bohun. I see, and I understand. You think yourself very sharp, and very cautious, but your silence betrays more than words would tell. However, my lady is listening to us, though she is smiling so sweetly on Captain Berrington, so let us talk of her instead of Hector. How well she looks by daylight."

"Extremely; it is that exceeding delicacy of complexion......"

"That's a cut at my brown cheeks."

"Pardon me, Miss Maynard. There are as many beautiful brunettes as blondes."

"Try again, Mr. Bohun; but you won't beat that in a hurry."

"I was about to observe that the first time I ever saw Lady Bohun was by daylight, and she struck me then as she strikes me now......"

"Where did you first see her?"

"At the Crystal Palace."

"If she stood the test of that glare, she can stand anything."

"She looked then as now—a perfectly beautiful young woman."

Miss Maynard gave a sigh.

"Well, do you know, Mr. Bohun, I am very glad."

"At what?"

"That you like her—didn't you say so?"

"You did not ask me, Miss Maynard."

"Bless the man and his evasions! never mind—but I am glad, because I like her myself. I like everything about her except......"

"An exception already?"

"Yes—except her maid. How can you and the vampire exist in the same air? Are you not afraid?"

"Do I look ill, Miss Maynard?"

"No, I don't think it has begun its deadly work yet......"

Mr. Bohun gave a shiver, and at that moment Lady Bohun suddenly addressed him—

"Somebody walking over your grave," said she with a smile.

"Two horrid prognostications in the course of

one second," whispered he to Miss Maynard, laughing.

" Captain Berrington," said Lady Bohun to her neighbour, who was an *habitué* at Bohun Court, " I think I must begin to try a little match-making. Do you think it would do ?" and she glanced at her brother-in-law and his tormentor.

" If matrimony ought to begin with a little antipathy, or even a great deal, it would do very well," was his answer.

" Why ? they have been whispering together all breakfast time."

" She on the offensive, and he on the defensive; that is all, Lady Bohun. Bohun is not the man to admire that style of girl. What do you think of her ?"

" I am amused. She is a character. I never saw any one like her."

" In this neighbourhood they are called ' the Maynards, *père et fils*.' Till you know her a little better, you will hardly appreciate the appropriate-ness of the phrase, but when you do, you will say she is well named Jem Maynard, for no other name would suit her. You did not know old Lady Merivale, did you, Lady Bohun ?"

" No, but I know she was a regular guest here in old days."

" Yes, and she was a marvellous old woman;
but what I was going to observe was, that when
people used to say to her they wondered that so
gentle, nervous, and delicate a person as the last
Lady Bohun, could put up with such a visitor as
Miss Maynard in the house, Lady Merivale used
to fire up in her defence and say, ' Why not? I
am sure she is very gentleman-like !' "

The trivial conversation of that breakfast table
sent Mr. Bohun to his den in a fit of profound
meditation. He had lived too long in the world
not to know that even in the most remote quarters, where the fewest possible number of people
are gathered together, those people will talk; but
human beings have very much of the ostrich in
their nature ; they hide their heads in the sand,
and flatter themselves they are invisible. Mr.
Bohun now saw that he had been hiding his,
whilst all his neighbours had been watching and
making remarks upon him.

" I want to know if you get on well together—
people say you don't."

That was the sentence that rung in his ears,
that had startled him when it was uttered, and
startled him still more now, when he sat quietly
down and dissected it. Even the consolatory
fumes of the forbidden cigar could not dissipate

the emotion with which he pulled that sentence
to pieces, and weighed every word of it.

Did they get on well together? Did his sister-
in-law—his brother's wife—and himself, get on
well together? that meant, did they agree?

They had lived under the same roof for three
months—had they ever had a quarrel? a dispute?
or an angry word?—never. But, nevertheless,
did they get on well together? Mr. Bohun looked
in the clear depths of Hector's large loving brown
eyes, upraised and fixed on his face, and seemed
to see the silent answer there. It was, no. Did
even they agree?—no; not in thought, or word,
or action; they had not a feeling, or a taste, in
common; no wonder then that they did not "get
on" together, much less "get on well."

And the world had found it out. This, to Mr.
Bohun, was the worst part of the business. For
the honour of the Bohun name, he would have
hidden the thorn in his heart for ever, had not
that same inquisitive world, that officious throng
called "people," of whom Miss Maynard was the
voice, drawn it to light.

And now, what could he do? he wanted somebody to talk to. He would have liked to have
gone down to the library and had a long chat with
Sir Felix, and to have said to him candidly, "I

want a home of my own—I want a *pied-à-terre*—
I am no longer of any particular use to you, since
stewards and bailiffs can do what I do much better
than myself. Let me go." But he well knew
that no sooner should he have seated himself to
have a *tête-à-tête* with his brother, than by some
mysterious agency, Lady Bohun would be informed of the fact, and would descend with a
long strip of work in her hand, express a little
surprise at finding him there, and seat herself in
the deep window, with the air of a martyr.

No—he could not go to Sir Felix. Then he
bethought him of his old friend the Rector—
he who, on the first rumour of the impending
marriage, had flown to him on the wings of true
friendship, to offer what now seemed to Mr.
Bohun to have been prophetic condolences. But
it was snowing heavily, and it was not worth
while running the risk of a wetting, and finding
the Rector out for the day.

There was but one other person with whom
Mr. Bohun was on terms to suit the present
moment. That was old Mrs. Trant. No chance
of her being out on such a day.

"Suppose we go and see Mrs. Trant, eh,
Hector?" said he.

The dog testified perfect acquiescence.

"We don't mind the snow, do we, Hector?"

And the huge animal was instantly on his feet, trembling with eager impatience, and a red light gleaming in his eyes. He knew he was going to be taken out for a run with his master.

"So we'll go, Hector," and drawing on high boots, and rolling himself in a plaid, Mr. Bohun and his dog sallied forth by the window.

CHAPTER XIV.

As he crossed the snow-covered lawn, Lady Bohun and Miss Maynard stood at a window which was at the extreme end of the gallery upstairs. They had been looking at the old family pictures, with a view of organising some *tableaux vivans.*

"There goes my knight," remarked the young lady; "what business has he to go out without me?"

"No hope of *our* stirring out such a day as this," said Lady Bohun, looking up at the leaden sky.

"Where can he have emerged from?" pursued Miss Maynard, "he and Hector?"

"From his 'den,' as he calls it," said Lady Bohun, rather contemptuously, "where they sit together all day, generally."

" But his den used to be up-stairs in my time; where is it now?"

" He has always inhabited the same rooms ever since I have known him," returned the young hostess, " a room at the end of the passage leading out of the great hall."

" Why that was the last Lady Bohun's own boudoir," exclaimed Miss Maynard, " and the nicest room in the house."

Euphemia said nothing; but coloured, and bit her lips.

" I know the room well," continued the fair Jem; " upon my word, Lady Bohun, you were very kind to give it up. Isn't it the very *beau-idéal* of a snuggery? and such an exquisite room in summer! Just under the window is an immense bed of lilies of the valley, the only place in the whole garden where they can be induced to flourish, and I always fancied the violets under that window were sweeter than anywhere else, not that I care for flowers particularly, only that room in your predecessor's time was the very Garden of Eden for fruits and flowers. Do let us go down, now that he is out, and rout out the bachelor's den, shall we?"

" Not for the world," said Lady Bohun. " Mr. Bohun smokes, and I assure you it is quite bad enough to pass even the end of the passage. I had a baize door put there before I had been a week in the house."

Miss Maynard laughed. "Poor dear! Did you really throw such cold water on its innocent little bachelor vice? Did he know why you put it up?"

"Of course he did; but what did that signify? He used to smoke in the conservatory, but I soon stopped that. I cannot well prevent his smoking in his own room, but I assure you my maid, whose window is just over that room, is half poisoned, and I am seriously thinking what can be done."

"You and I would never do to live together, then," laughed her companion, "for I go halves in all my old father's cigars. But, now, what can we do to amuse ourselves? How infamous of that man to go out! Never mind; let us find Captain Berrington and some more of the gentlemen, and go and have a game of billiards, shall we?"

"But the ladies?" said Euphemia, "I must try and amuse them."

"Don't. You are not bound to look after them till after luncheon. Leave them with their novels."

Miss Maynard was as good as her word. She found the gentlemen, as many as had not ventured out, and played at billiards with them till luncheon. The snow continued to descend heavily, and the carriages that had been ordered to take away a few of the guests were counter-manded. Every one looked fearfully at the weather, for there was a fair prospect of being snowed up, and the afternoon closed in, dull and dark, before four o'clock. It was at this crisis that Miss Maynard came out in brilliant colours. In the evening they were to have *tableaux,* but how to spend the time from four till seven?

"Shut up," cried Miss Maynard, "shut the shutters, clear a large table, and let us have a round game."

And sure enough, when Sir Felix entered the drawing-room just before the first dinner bell rang, he found almost all his guests in the midst of an uproarious game of lansquenet.

Never before had the sober walls of Bohun Court looked down on such a sight! But as Eu-phemia seemed as much amused as any of the party, Sir Felix retired to his own precincts again with a satisfied smile on his face, and there he sat till she joined him, dressed for dinner.

She had something to say to him. He always

read this in the manner in which she used to enter the library, and it generally made him feel a little nervous. He never knew what might be coming.

The fact was, she had been holding a conversation with Ponsford during the process of adornment, and a visit to Sir Felix was invariably the result of these conversations.

Ever since the morning Lady Bohun had been brooding over what Miss Maynard had told her about Mr. Bohun's having taken possession of the late Lady Bohun's boudoir! but she had no opportunity till the evening of exhaling all the annoyance it had caused her. To Ponsford, however, every grievance was sure to be immediately detailed, because they met with such ready sympathy.

"Ponsford, did you know that that room appropriated by Mr. Bohun down-stairs was always the boudoir in this house?"

"Oh! yes, my lady. It is the prettiest room in the house, and the sunniest, which was the reason the late Lady Bohun always inhabited it."

"Why did you never tell me so, Ponsford?"

Ponsford looked surprised. She thought, of course, her ladyship knew it.

"Indeed, I did not. I always imagined that

the small drawing-room—the room *I* call the boudoir—was Lady Bohun's."

"No, my lady. Her ladyship was very delicate, and required the morning sun. That is the only room in the house that seems always to have the sun, yet never to be too warm, so her ladyship quite lived in it."

"No wonder. I am sure I am perished in the drawing-rooms. I had no idea that there was a more comfortable room than the one that has been fitted up for me. Mr. Bohun seems to have feathered his nest very completely, I must say! I never thought of there being a pretty room down that dark narrow passage."

"There is a door into the drawing-rooms, my lady, and that used to be open in former times."

"You must be mistaken, Ponsford. There can be no door of communication, or I should surely have seen it."

"Indeed, begging your ladyship's pardon, there is. Lady Bohun used to be wheeled right through all the rooms twice a day, when she became too ill to go out."

"Then that room actually belongs to the suite, then?"

"That it certainly does, my lady."

"Well! that is pretty cool of a bachelor, I

think, isn't it? But I think you must be mistaken about the door, Ponsford."

" Well, my lady, it may certainly have been bricked up......"

"Oh! dear no; there are no signs of such a thing."

" Then, my lady, it is behind that large carved ebony cabinet......I know that is where it always was."

Lady Bohun fell into a reverie.

"I must see about this," said she, half-talking to herself, and when Ponsford had put the finishing stroke to her toilette, she descended to the library.

Ostensibly, she went there to await the ringing of the second dinner bell (the custom of Bohun Court being to ring three), but, in reality, to follow her favourite custom of striking whilst the iron was hot. Mr. Bohun must not remain in undisturbed possession of that room if she could help it. The assumption of it amounted to a positive impertinence; but how to begin was rather a difficulty. Fortunately, Sir Felix led to it himself. He thought Euphemia must be fagged to death with her guests; it had been a long day for everybody, but more trying, of course, to the hostess than to her friends, particularly as all these guests were comparative strangers.

"Miss Maynard, that extraordinary girl," said Euphemia, in reply, "has been a great assistance to me—Ponsford said she would be. But I confess I should feel less fatigue if I had some warm little snug room to retreat into. Dear Sir Felix, the cold to-day has been intense. Is it possible you have not felt it?"

"I cannot say I have. I was obliged to ride over to the horse-fair, and came home very far from cold, I assure you. Guy generally arranges the farm purchases for me, but to-day, as ill-luck would have it, he was out of the way—not to be found anywhere. But, my dear Euphemia, after all the pains I took, I should be extremely vexed if the boudoir I prepared with so much care for you, were deficient in luxury or comfort. What is it you wish? You know you have only to give your orders—tell me how it can be made more comfortable?"

"Oh! dear Sir Felix, it is not the furniture, or the luxury, or the comfort, that I care for so much as the situation and aspect of the room. In the first place, it is what I call a passage room; actually it has three doors—one from the hall, one from the drawing-rooms, one from the dining-room."

"My dearest, that is one of the peculiarities in

the construction and arrangement of Bohun Court.
You may walk round the entire circle of the hall
through all the rooms; every room is what you
call a passage room."

"Yes, but every room has not three doors, Sir
Felix. Three doors make a boudoir something
like an ice-house. Three doors and a fire-place!
I wonder sometimes I do not catch my death of
cold."

Sir Felix smiled, for during the whole course
of his acquaintance with the fair Euphemia, he
had never seen her with anything approaching
a cold.

"Ah! you may laugh," said she, testily, "but
if you sat there as much as I do, you would not
like it. Besides, there is no retirement in that
room; guests in the drawing-room can hear every
word I say; and as for the sun, I never see it till
two or three o'clock, and then in summer I shall
be burnt up there."

Sir Felix leant back in his chair, with his hand
over his mouth in an attitude of meditation,
Euphemia glancing at him out of the corners of
her eyes, watching her moment.

"I understand," said she, cautiously, "that
that was not originally the boudoir."

"No......no......" hesitated Sir Felix, "certainly

it was not; but it occurred to me that this would make you such a pretty room, because of the view. The other has no view."

"What other?"

"Guy's little room; that was the boudoir in old days."

"So I am told," said Euphemia, coldly.

Something in her voice struck Sir Felix, and he looked up hastily, but the words he seemed about to utter died away.

It was Lady Bohun who continued.

"And Mr. Bohun has taken it for his own room, I hear."

"Yes," said Sir Felix, briefly.

"Temporarily or for a continuance? For as long as he lives here?"

"My dear Euphemia," exclaimed her husband, at last rousing from his placidity, "this house is my brother's home."

Strong language, thought the young wife, but it did not daunt her. It was a point of too deep annoyance for that.

"I am aware of that," she rejoined; "but is he to appropriate the nicest room in the house to the sacrifice of my comfort?"

"Dearest Euphemia, have you seen it? Have you really carefully surveyed the little apartment you seem to covet? Believe me, it will not bear a shadow of comparison with your own boudoir, and whoever has told you so, has, I fear, had some mischievous motive for such exaggeration. My brother requested me, as a favour, to allow him to have that room—he had a peculiar and touching interest in it. I could no more have found the heart to deny him that request, than I could now have the courage to ask him to resign it."

"Oh, dear!" laughed Lady Bohun, satirically, "if *you* do not possess the courage, Sir Felix, *I do!* I assure you I should ask it as easily as possible, but, mark me, not to be refused! If you give me authority to request him to change rooms with me, the request must be complied with!"

"That depends upon my brother, Euphemia."

"You are not, then, master in your own house, Sir Felix?"

"Not to the cost of Guy's comfort, my dear Euphemia."

"My comfort, then, is of secondary importance to you?"

"My dearest, I have done everything in my power to endeavour to ensure it."

"And the first favour I ask you, you refuse?"

"Ask me anything but this, Euphemia. I gave

my brother my word that nothing should disturb his tenancy of that room. He is attached to it, and his reasons are sacred to me. My dearest, you possess my whole affection as a living wife, but the dead must at least claim my respect. I cannot eject Guy from his occupation of that boudoir, so do not grieve me by saying you have asked it as a favour."

"But I have, Sir Felix!" cried Euphemia, her eyes flashing fire; "and, moreover, I have been denied. Thank you," she added, rising haughtily, "I thank you for making me nominal mistress of a house with two masters! But remember, Sir Felix, however much consideration and obedience *you* may please to show Mr. Bohun, *I* owe him none, nor will I pay him any. It is quite bad enough to have an idle bachelor living in one's house......"

"Euphemia, Euphemia!" exclaimed Sir Felix, his voice trembling with agitation. "I beseech you not to utter words which, in a cooler moment, you will feel are both cruel and unjust!"

"Not I! If he is to interfere with me and my happiness, I will, at any rate, let him know it!"

"Euphemia, you shock me! The idea of Guy, so good, so amiable, so unoffending......"

" Ah, yes ! so perfect and so delightful ! No wonder he deserves to be petted ! But, my dear Sir Felix, he has not been good, and amiable, and unoffending to *me!* Remember that odious dog the very first day after I arrived."

" He withdrew it the moment you objected."

" Withdrew it from our breakfast and dinner table, certainly; but does it not still go on howling every moonlight night till it drives me nearly wild ?"

" If that is the case, Euphemia, I will try for a remedy by asking Guy to send it down to the kennels."

" Asking Guy, indeed ! Why not send it, since it annoys me ?"

" It shall be seen to," said Sir Felix, wearily.

" Then that disgusting smoking !"

" Oh ! my dearest, you have nothing to complain of there ! My brother most studiously and scrupulously avoids smoking near any of your rooms."

" He smokes in his own, which is just under Ponsford's, and she is half poisoned. She cannot actually open her window during the hours he indulges in a habit which makes a man totally unfit for ladies' society. This is another reason why I wish his room to be altered. If Ponsford

takes my dresses into her room for any alterations,
they come back to me fragrant with that intolerable
smoke! Is this to be borne?"

"My dear Euphemia," exclaimed Sir Felix,
rising hastily, as the third dinner bell pealed
through the house, "everything you have said
shall be carefully weighed by me, and remedies
found if possible; but I cannot consent to any
plan which involves the discomfort of my brother."

"You repeat, then, that you don't mind mine?"

"I never said so at all; but, my dearest Euphemia, prove, by your silence to Guy on these
subjects, that you have some confidence in me; trust
to my devotion to your happiness, and spare my
brother the pang of feeling that he is not now as
much at home in this house as he has been for
forty years—spare him this, and everything you
wish shall be arranged."

"Oh, skeleton in my cupboard!" ejaculated
Lady Bohun to herself, as, decking her face in
its usual smiles, she preceeded her husband to
the drawing-room, and prepared, with apparent
sweetness and inward bitterness, to go the round
of her guests; "skeleton in my cupboard, you
shall be a rod in my hand over that weak man,
to mould him to my will! Mistress will I be in
this house, or my name is not Lady Bohun!"

CHAPTER XV.

AND in this mood she took her place at the head of her brilliant table.

Are there not many, and many, and many of us, who sit at our festive boards, mix smilingly in our gay circles, and go cheerfully about the world, doing our every-day work of pleasure or business, with these self-same skeletons in our hearts? Is there one bosom so full of happiness, or so free from care, that it holds no place in which the grim visitor may not, at some time or other, take his ghastly seat? perhaps not all with equal ghastliness, but still, is he not there, dim and undefined, or else, mighty in silent power?

A bitter, vengeful skeleton haunted Lady Bohun through every room of her house, and a restless, anxious dread was the skeleton that had now begun to prey on the mind of Sir Felix. In another bosom, too, at that table, sat the spectre,

gleaming sadly from the thoughtful forehead of
Mr. Bohun, and " waiting by his side." Even he
had, at last, bowed down before it. It seemed as
though, having just effected an entrance into
Bohun Court, it was appearing before the different
inmates of the old place in various shapes.

At all events, there was a skeleton in the
house, but outwardly, the merry party went on
all the same.

People talked, and laughed, and demolished all
the good things, and Lady Bohun talked and
laughed more than anyone else. She carried it
off well ; but Mr. Bohun sat far back in his chair
and hardly answered the lively sallies of Miss
Maynard. As for Sir Felix, he had that day
handed to dinner a new lady-resident of the
neighbourhood, who rose from table with the
impression that she had never sat next to so
stupid a person in her life.

And she who had caused this disquietude,
.secretly watched, with scarcely concealed satisfaction, the working of her spells, although to the ·
ear of the assembled guests she was but planning
the *tableaux* for the evening.

There was a buoyant sort of gaiety in the
manner of Lady Bohun which was very fascina-
ting to casual acquaintances, and to Sir Felix it

was witchery itself. The consequence was, that whilst listening to her, and admiring her, he entirely forgot that it was her hand that had planted the thorn which was festering at his heart, but felt much more inclined to lay the blame elsewhere.

" Yes," thought he to himself, as he answered all his neighbours' questions wrong, "yes, it is hard to bring a young girl from her home to live amongst utter strangers, and not to exert every nerve to make her happy. It is hard for her to make requests, and to have them refused. I feel for her, poor young thing, and I was harsh, almost cruel, not instantly to accede to her wishes. Happily, with the elasticity of her youth and spirits, she seems to have forgotten it; but this very evening, if I can speak to Guy, it shall be all altered."

Did not that young wife know perfectly what was passing in her husband's mind? Yes, as perfectly as if he had spoken for all the room to hear, so she "bided her time" patiently, convinced that, in the end, she would gain her point, though, at present, things looked unpropitious.

Miss Maynard, as usual, sat by Mr. Bohun at dinner, and attacked him on the subject of his absence from home that day.

" And my only morning here, as far as you knew," said she, " for we little expected to be snowed up. However, we have spent a most agreeable day—I have won fifteen shillings at lansquenet, and a box of cigars at billiards from young Montgomery. He offered to play for gloves, but I said cigars were more in my line, and I won them."

" Young Montgomery," as the fair Jem called a gentleman who sat opposite to her, was a tall, pale individual, with a glass in his eye, one of those sort of people who might be any age between twenty and fifty, which, perhaps, was the reason that he always went by the name of " young Montgomery."

" With such attractive amusements," was Mr. Bohun's answer, " I hope you did not miss me as much as might be expected."

" Yes, we did, because we happened to want you. So shabby of you to leave us when there was so much to be arranged. Nobody could find the key of the old cabinet at the end of the gallery, where Ponsford......(you know......the vampire......) said there were some ancient court dresses......"

" How did she know?" asked Mr. Bohun, very abruptly.

" Because she knows everything; so the cry for Mr. Bohun was universal, was it not, Lady Bohun?"

" I beg your pardon?" said Euphemia, interrogatively, smiling sweetly, pretending not to hear but having heard every word.

" Did we not want Mr. Bohun, at luncheon, about our *tableaux?*"

" But he was at luncheon, was he not?" said Lady Bohun, with a look of feigned surprise.

" Unhappy man, to be so little missed!" laughed Miss Maynard, and there was a sudden silence round the table.

It might have been accident, it might have been intentional, but, certainly, these " awful pauses" do invariably occur at awkward moments, and so it was in the present case. Lady Bohun kept her eyes fixed on her plate—Sir Felix set his face very stiffly—and over Mr. Bohun's calm and chiselled countenance there came a flush, but no other sign of annoyance.

Old Mr. Melville, the rector of Bohun, happened to be at table that day, and something in this incident, trivial as it was, seemed to strike him. He glanced uneasily at Mr. Bohun, and this glance caught Mr. Bohun's eye, bringing back to his memory again Miss Maynard's ex-

pression of the evening before—those careless
words, " People say you don't."

" Ah," thought he to himself, " everybody sees
it, everybody knows it, even old Melville, poor,
good old man !"

But Miss Maynard went on. "I will tell you
what our first *tableaux* is to be. Queen Elizabeth giving the ring to the Earl of Essex. We
wanted you to stand for Essex."

" Not to your Queen Elizabeth, Miss Maynard."

" Why not, Mr. Bohun ?"

" Because I am so often offending you that the
ring would be coming back every day."

" Well, as it happens, Lady Bohun is the
Queen, and she may be a more forgiving person
than I am; however, it is all settled now, with
young Montgomery as Essex, so you are out of
it, but you had no business to be out of the way
when we wanted you, had he, Lady Bohun ?"

" I think we have done pretty well," said the
hostess, in a very gentle voice; "at least, I hope
everybody will say so."

" Yes," persisted Miss Maynard, " only no one
knows all the nooks and crannies of this dear old
house as Mr. Bohun does, and, by the by, we
still want some armour."

" Sir Felix," said Lady Bohun, again, very gently, but distinctly and pointedly, " we shall want you, after dinner, to show us some suitable armour for our second *tableaux*—Edward receiving the keys of Calais."

Whilst Sir Felix was replying, Miss Maynard lowered her voice to a whisper.

" Mr. Bohun, I want to scold you. You and I are old friends, and I take liberties accordingly. Do you know that you are behaving very badly? Why don't you conciliate that sweet creature more ?"

" What sweet creature, Miss Maynard ? Young Montgomery ?"

"Pshaw ! nonsense ! you know who I mean; and what I mean, too. I think her charming."

" I am delighted to hear it, Miss Maynard."

" Then why are you so cold? so distant? so reserved? with your ' Lady Bohun,' and her ' Mr. Bohun,' and your cat and dog looks at each other? why don't you call her Euphemia (though it certainly is the most frightful name that ever parent inflicted on a child), and then she would call you Guy."

" I have almost forgotten that such is my name, Miss Maynard. When we grow old, we drop our names, and take to our titles."

"Stuff! If I were Duchess of Diamond-eyes, no soul would ever dream of calling me anything but Jem, unless yourself. But you have grown so stiff; you are a perfect ogre. I don't know you now, Mr. Bohun, and let me tell you privately as a friend, that it is not wise of you—not politic —she is an important personage, and you are a bear—now don't fire up, but give me some of those brandy cherries."

Oh, careless words! careless words! do the speakers of careless words ever think them over again afterwards, and repeat them to themselves? sift them? weigh them? and see what amount of pain, grief, or vexation their utterance may have inflicted?

No, seldom; scarcely ever, perhaps never; so never till that last great day, when our thoughts will sound in our ears like words, and when our words will stand before us like deeds, shall we ever know or see, what gaping wounds these same light careless words have made. Then shall we see where the sword stabbed and the blow bruised, but till then, no doubt we shall go on all the same —evil-speaking, lying, and slandering—harsh sounding sins, but all committed under the specious cloak of " careless words !"

Almost every sentence that Miss Maynard had

spoken that day at dinner, had contained something in it to pain or annoy Mr. Bohun, and her last was the climax.

What was not wise? what was not politic? why, in his own home, was he to be wise? why, under his own brother's roof, was he obliged to be politic? and if so, what was to be his particular line of policy? conciliatory? that implied a want of present, cordiality, and how did Miss Maynard know that cordiality did *not* exist between this important personage and himself?

How indeed? how but because "people" said so!

The ladies rose just as Mr. Bohun was saying to himself, "This is all very uncomfortable," and he found his next neighbour was then old Mr. Melville, a congenial spirit under the circumstances.

Yet he too began in a somewhat similar strain; complaining of how little he had seen of his friend of late.

"Then," said Mr. Bohun, "I suppose what all the world says must be true, and I am really growing morose and ogreish; but upon my word I have taken precisely the same walks at the same hours, paid the same visits, and sat in my room exactly in the same place for the last four months, as I have for the last four years—how then can these accusations be just?"

"I have been wishing to speak to you on many matters connected with the parish," began Mr. Melville; "in the first place, about repairing the interior of the church. I have been calculating that we might collect a very handsome sum in subscriptions, if I might head the list by your name and that of Sir Felix......"

"We are always ready, my dear sir," interrupted Mr. Bohun, "but let me beg of you to lay the matter first before my brother and Lady Bohun."

"I know that is the proper course," returned the old Rector; "but you are aware, dear Mr. Bohun, that we are all so much in the habit of appealing to you as our fountain-head, that any departure from the old established custom, seems to me quite like an omission."

"Thank you for the compliment, old friend," said Mr. Bohun; "but let it be understood from henceforth, that it is not pleasant for me to be drawn from the retirement which I have chosen; in fact, I am nobody here now, and I must not be consulted first on points like these."

"I am sorry, but you shall be obeyed, because you are right," was the Rector's reply; "only, dear sir, it never *was* so, and I certainly had hoped things would have remained on the same footing as formerly. It is a disappointment to me."

Here again! Mr. Bohun could bear it no longer. He turned himself towards Mr. Melville on his chair, and throwing his arm over the back of it, at once dashed into his subject.

"My good old friend, you are not the first person who has used similar words to me this day. I have spent all this snowy morning with Mrs. Trant, and we have had a long and serious conversation on my present position at Bohun Court. You are quite correct in saying that things are no longer on the same footing as formerly. It is perfectly true; so much so, that I consulted Mrs. Trant very earnestly to-day, as to whether it would not be much better for me no longer to make this house my home......"

·The Rector started.

"Yes," continued Mr. Bohun, "I consulted her because I have great confidence in her judgment, as also in yours, my dear friend; so, after her, I was coming to you."

"What did Mrs. Trant say?" asked the old man anxiously.

"She was against any change at present."

"So am I," exclaimed Mr. Melville, without a moment's hesitation. "So am I, decidedly."

"On what grounds?"

"Because Bohun Court cannot do without you."

"That was not Mrs. Trant's reason."

"What then?"

"She was of opinion that, for my brother's sake, in the eyes of the world, it would be more—more......"

"Politic," suggested the Rector. (Miss Maynard's objectionable word!)

"It would look better," modified Mr. Bohun, "that no change were made at present; but I confess this is not my opinion. I think he (or she) who takes up his residence with a newly-married couple, commits a great mistake, and that mistake I have made. I see it, and I am ready to rectify it. My only hesitation is, from what Mrs. Trant said this morning, that various unpleasant rumours as to discord within the walls of Bohun Court are just now afloat, and that the best contradiction that could be given to them would be, my continued stay here."

"True, true, very true!" sighed Mr. Melville.

"But my mind is not made up," continued Mr. Bohun, "and until I have consulted with my brother, I can come to no resolution. I did consult with him just before his marriage. I represented to him that if only for my own comfort, I wished him to let me leave him......"

"And he could not spare you? no, nor can we, Mr. Bohun."

"Mr. Melville, you must remember that my brother is a very easy man, disliking anything like business or trouble, and hitherto I have certainly been able to save him from both, partly from circumstances during his married life, but still more from his long absences from home, and his positive refusal to attend to the estate during his widowhood. The fact is, that I have been so pushed into the foreground, my dear sir, that I actually find it difficult to be beaten back," and Mr. Bohun laughed half bitterly, half good-humouredly.

"Well," said the Rector, "now that *you* have spoken, let *me* speak. As to being beaten back, I trust it may never, never, come to that."

"Exactly—but I wish to retire before there is a chance of it."

"Then as to Sir Felix; the same disinclination for business which he has always shown, still clings to him. If you leave Bohun Court, it will be thrown upon the hands of servants or stewards, and then......"

" Pardon me," interrupted Mr. Bohun, with a touch of *hauteur* which very rarely appeared in his manner to any one, much less to this, his oldest friend, " pardon me, but in that case, everything will be in the hands of Lady Bohun."

" And is that wise ?" asked Mr. Melville.

" What do you mean ?" questioned Mr. Bohun, in his turn, recalling instantly Miss Maynard's mysterious warning words, and seeing now the prospect of their solution; " how do you mean that it is not wise ?"

" My dear friend," exclaimed the old man, energetically, " when a man at your brother's time of life falls into the hands of a young wife, woe betide him who has been looked upon all his life as heir presumptive !"

Mr. Bohun drew a very long breath. " That's it, is it ?" said he ; " that, then, is what people mean by my not being wise, and not being politic ? My neighbours imagine that I live under my brother's roof to be a spy upon his actions, and for the sake of what I can get ! My dear friend, if it has come to this, it is, indeed, high time that I should go."

" You have taken a wrong view of the case,"

said the Rector; "what we mean is, that there may be no heirs to Bohun Court. In that case, though your position remains what it has ever been, your interests, under present circumstances, require more looking after."

Mr. Bohun laughed.

"You all amuse me," said he, "you speak out so openly; but can you possibly think that Sir Felix would marry a young wife, and not leave her everything he had in the world?"

"Everything, save Bohun Court," exclaimed Mr. Melville, hastily; "he has so often spoken to me of his devotion to this old place, and of *your* devotion to it, and his fears that no lady would ever appreciate it, and take the care he or you would wish taken of it, that I cannot conceive its passing from you. Suppose now for instance, the widow were to marry again?"

"What good can I do, or what harm can I prevent, by overlooking in the lifetime of the rightful owners?"

"Many things; for instance, supposing you were in the direct line to inherit, should you like any trees about here cut down?"

"Certainly not; but ladies don't often interfere with the timber on an estate."

"Just before this frost I happened to be resting on a bank outside Bohun Woods; Lady Bohun and her maid were standing very near me; accidentally I overheard the conversation. Lady Bohun was lamenting the thickness of the firs, and wishing to have more open views of the house; her maid was marking trees with a piece of chalk......"

Mr. Bohun pinched in his lips. "No orders have been given for any trees to be cut down," said he, temperately; but any one could have seen by the expression of his face that such an act would be next to drawing his own life blood.

"The next words I heard were, how much better Bohun Court would look whitewashed."

"Who said that?" cried Mr. Bohun, his eyes lighting up with a flash like fire.

"The maid."

"And Lady Bohun......?"

"Lady Bohun perfectly agreed."

The disgust on Mr. Bohun's face was almost ludicrous from its intensity, but he said nothing. He pushed back his chair, and rose.

"Well?" inquired his old friend, "now do you think it better to go or stay!"

"Stay," was the laconic reply.

"I thought so. It is wisest."

"You are right," returned Mr. Bohun, "it *is*

wisest; but if any further remarks are made, remember, old friend, that I stay from wisdom, not policy; I stay to preserve Bohun Court from desecration, not for any advantage *I* can gain, for, as I said before, it is absurd to imagine that from the moment Sir Felix married a young wife, any soul but that young wife would have either part or parcel in his worldly goods and chattels. Besides," he added, lightly, as the guests proceeded into the drawing-room, "we shall most likely hear the sound of merry little voices, and the tread of nimble little feet through the galleries of Bohun Court before many years have passed away, and then, what will have been the use of all my wisdom, and all my policy?"

"Wait till you hear them," said the Rector, prophetically; "wait; but Bohun Court never heard them yet, and never may; so all I say is, wait !"

CHAPTER XVI.

THE old house was snowed up for many days, and the prisoner-guests amused themselves as best they could. Lady Bohun and Miss Maynard led the revels, and when at last a bright, cheery morning dawned, and nothing of the snow was left save a patch here and there in a shady corner, people were half sorry.

" As for me," said Miss Maynard, " I am grieved. I never enjoyed a visit more. Don't you regret the snow, Lady Bohun ?"

" Not I," exclaimed the young lady ; " I hate snow. It makes this house look like a large hearse. I never saw snow lie so heavily anywhere in my life. It shows how cold the situation is."

Two reflections upon Bohun Court in one sentence, thought somebody in the room.

" In what happy hemisphere may you have

resided, never to have seen a heavier fall than
this?" asked young Montgomery, who was lounging in the recess of the next window.

"I have seen many a heavier fall," retorted
Lady Bohun; " but papa never allowed the snow
to lie about *our* grounds, that is what I meant."

" Ah !" said Miss Maynard, carelessly, "it is
easier to sweep up a lawn than such an extent of
park as this."

" Only the lawn at *my* home happens to be of
greater extent than the park here," was Lady
Bohun's answer, whilst the colour rushed into her
cheeks.   She had a great dislike to any one
imagining that she had not been used to quite as
much luxury at home, if not more, than she had
found at Bohun Court.

"Berrington," whispered Mr. Montgomery,
" where has the beautiful simpleton lived all her
life ?"

" Oh ! in some London suburb."

" Cockney villa, eh ?"

"I think so, only on a very large scale.   The
father is a man of immense wealth."

" Then she doesn't know how to appreciate an-
tiquities."

" Not she.   She despises this mouldy old mansion."

Mr. Bohun heard all but the first sentence, and by the colour in Euphemia's face he fancied she had also, and came immediately to the rescue.

" Lady Bohun," said he, clearly and distinctly, " you must introduce some modern improvements amongst us. We must strike you as quite benighted after the state of perfection to which ornamental gardening has been brought in *your* home. I ˜assure you, when my brother came down here after a certain memorable visit to town, or rather its neighbourhood, he called everything at Bohun Court dingy !"

Miss Maynard came behind him and pinched his arm.

" Well done," she whispered; "now that I call generous and magnificent of you."

But Euphemia had not any of those finer feelings which would have appreciated generosity of this kind. She only saw in the remarks of her brother-in-law a proper admission of the inferiority of Bohun Court to The Laurels, and her eyes sparkled triumphantly as she laughed and answered,

"Oh! we taught Sir Felix a good deal I dare say, though I cannot say he has profited much. However, that does not signify, for I assure you I am only waiting for a little fine

weather to set seriously to work and completely
new-model Bohun Court."

"Look, how aghast Mr. Bohun stands," whispered Miss Maynard again, but this time the
whisper was to the young hostess.

"Why?" exclaimed Euphemia, opening her
eyes, "what on earth is it *to him!*"

The look, the air, the intonation, all spoke volumes, and Miss Maynard felt the question unanswerable, though it was to those who heard it a
painful truth. It was, indeed, nothing now to
him, and the day might come when it would be
even less. Were the little feet and the little
voices ever to sound through the polished oak
galleries of that old house, it would be nothing
more to him than the memory of a dream.

And now the guests were all gone, and Sir
Felix and Lady Bohun were left, not exactly to
themselves, but with only "the third person," as
Euphemia had now actually begun to speak of
Mr. Bohun to Ponsford.

It then occurred to Sir Felix that he had made
his young wife some sort of promise, that day of the
theatricals, which he had not yet performed, and
one morning he screwed up his courage—yes, it
required screwing up—to speak to his brother
as they sat over a heap of business papers, about

the various grievances which she had laid before him. He resolved to begin upon the least first.

" Guy, my dear fellow, I wanted, by the by, whilst I think of it, to ask you about Hector; has he not grown rather more noisy than usual?"

" Not that I have observed," replied his brother.

" Well, it strikes me he has. I don't recollect ever having heard him howl at night so much before."

" Has he really been howling? He bays at the moon on bright nights, I know, but I have not heard him howl. I am a good sleeper certainly, but a howl from Hector would wake me in a moment."

" The face of his kennel is toward our windows, perhaps that may have something to do with it."

" It shall be turned."

" I doubt if that would make it much better; Euphemia is a very light sleeper, and has been sadly disturbed by him lately, only, knowing your affection for the dog—and indeed, mine too—she has forborne complaining."

Mr. Bohun was silent for a few minutes, and a shadow came across his face.

" What does Lady Bohun wish?" said he, at last.

" It is I who am agitating the question, my

dear Guy," returned Sir Felix, nervously, as well
as evasively ; " I who am trying to see what can
be done, not Euphemia."

" Yes, I understand," said Mr. Bohun, coldly.

Sir Felix began to tear a pen to pieces. He
felt and looked extremely nervous, more so than
his brother had. ever seen him; so much so, indeed, that Mr. Bohun sat and looked at him sor-
rowfully, and then for the first time he saw that a
change had come over him, and that he had aged
ten years since he had come down to Bohun
Court one short year before, and announced his
intended marriage.

So Mr. Bohun sat and looked in sorrow and
pity.

"Felix," said he, at last, "you don't look well.
You look worried."

" And so I am," was the candid and abrupt
reply.

" About what?"

" About fifty things."

" Not about Hector surely ?"

" Yes, he is amongst the fifty."

" You wish him sent down to the kennels?"

" Would you object to it ?"

" Of course you know that if he goes there I
lose my companion. He looks for his two walks

a-day with me as regularly as clock-work, but if he is sent a mile away, I must cut off one of these, and that, I suspect, will make him howl in reality."

Sir Felix saw a loop-hole. "If the wind sets this way," said he, quickly, "we hear the dogs down at the kennels distinctly."

"We certainly do," said Mr. Bohun.

"Then I will tell Euphemia so," exclaimed his brother, much relieved; "and I have no doubt she will then prefer matters remaining as they are."

Mr. Bohun concealed a smile. It amused him in a painful sort of way, to see the reign of thraldom which had just begun to dawn on the husband of six months; it was something new, so entirely new, that Mr. Bohun could hardly realize it, although its effects were always presenting themselves before his eyes. The worst part of it was that it seemed to be affecting his brother's health. Had it not been for that, he would have laughed it to scorn; as it was, he tried how a little cheerfulness would do.

"Come," said he, gaily "you have only told me of one trouble, and there are forty-nine left. Having settled one, let us get on to the next."

But instead of answering in the same spirit,

Sir Felix, to Mr. Bohun's great surprise, suddenly hid his face in his hands.

"Oh, Guy, Guy!" he exclaimed; "there are times when I feel as if I had more troubles than I can talk of, even to you. I don't know what has come to me. I feel unhinged, shaky, not myself; and yet if you ask me to put these troubles into a tangible form, I cannot. Things worry me now that never used to worry me in old days, and I get one thought into my mind sometimes, which preys on it for days and days, and wears me to a shadow, mind and body."

"Have you such a thought now?" asked Mr. Bohun.

"Yes," was the answer, and there was a dead silence. In the midst of it, there was a slight rustle at the door.

"Lady Bohun!" exclaimed Sir Felix, under his voice, and flushing up very red.

His brother rose, and opened the door quickly. There was no one there.

"No one, Guy?"

"No one to be seen."

"How strange. I certainly fancied......however, it must have been fancy."

"A fancy I shared with you, Felix. But to return to our subject. You were speaking of a thought sometimes preying on your mind, and haunting you for days and days; this is a morbid state in which you ought not to indulge......" .

"Indulge? Good heavens! Do you suppose such an incubus is any indulgence?"

"I mean that it is weak of you to suffer a painful thought to master you. Rouse yourself, and dispel the dream."

"If it were a dream, I could do so. It is no dream. It is a reality."

"And a mystery, apparently, for I do not understand you."

The eyes of Sir Felix glanced towards the door; he seemed about to speak, then seemed to hesitate, change his mind, and finally relapsed into his former state.

"I don't think you are well," said Mr. Bohun at last, having for some time attentively regarded him in unbroken silence.

"Perhaps not."

"Would not a little change do you good?"

"Where could I go?"

"The idea! why, anywhere, everywhere, for change of scene, if not for change of air. You never used to think anything of running up to town a little while ago?"

"Ah! moving *en garçon*, and moving with a

retinue, are two very different things. I have
had so much moving, so much trouble and worry,
and fatigue, for the last six months, that really I
dread the very name of a journey now."

"But why not run up for a day or two by
yourself?"

Sir Felix hesitated.

"You would soon get rid of this thought of
yours," pursued Mr. Bohun; but his brother
shook his head wearily.

"Will you go?" asked Mr. Bohun, abruptly.

"I have a good deal to talk about before I think
of a journey for recreation," at last answered Sir
Felix, "and we may not have so good an opportunity for some time. The next question I
wanted to ask you was about your......"

"But Felix, will you first tell me what harasses
you? Don't leave that subject for a new one."

"We can go back to that, Guy."

"No time like the present, my good brother."

At that instant the door suddenly opened, but
till we retrace our steps half-an-hour, the intruder
must remain un-named.

Lady Bohun had been sitting in her boudoir,
the octagon, as it was still called, and being a
person of no pursuits, had found time hanging
very heavy on the hands which could neither

play, nor draw, nor work, unless the everlasting strip which never advanced an inch, could be dignified by the latter name.

The house was very quiet that day. She was wondering where Sir Felix could be. She was puzzling to think if she could not find some excuse to ring for Ponsford, anything, in fact, for company, and to kill time, when there came at the door a peculiar little rap—a rap like finger nails, not the usual rap with the knuckles.

"Come in, Ponsford," said her ladyship, and the lady's-maid obeyed. "Well?"

Ponsford's appearance, unsummoned, was always indicative of some secret intelligence.

"My lady, Sir Felix and Mr. Bohun have been in the library together for more than an hour. I happened to be drying your ladyship's flowers in the hall."

"I thought so! I suspected as much!" exclaimed Euphemia; "and alone, of course."

"Oh, yes, my lady!"

"What were they talking about?"

"I think it was about the farms, my lady, and the renovating of the church, but they came to Hector at last."

"At last! You may well say at last! And so Sir Felix has actually recollected that abomin-

able dog at last! Well, what did Mr. Bohun
say? Is anything settled?"

"Oh, yes, my lady!" said Ponsford, with her
gentle laugh; "settled in a very few sentences,
by Mr. Bohun. Hector is not to go away."

Lady Bohun coloured crimson. "And who
said so, pray?"

"Sir Felix did his utmost, my lady; but indeed,
as your ladyship will surely see some day, Mr.
Bohun always had, and always will have, his own
way. Sir Felix thought the dog had better be
sent to the kennels, but Mr. Bohun thought not,
and so the matter ended."

"But the matter has *not* ended," cried Euphemia, starting up; " when it ends, it shall be
in a very different way. Give me my strip of
work, Ponsford—quick!—and my thimble. What
more did you hear?"

" Just as Sir Felix was going to say something
very particular, my lady, and just as Mr. Bohun
was drawing him out, as it were, the hall door
opened, and the wind came rushing up, and blew
my dress against the library door, upon which Mr.
Bohun rose like a shot......"

" And you were discovered?"

" Oh, dear no, my lady!"—Ponsford's laugh was
a little sarcastic this time—" besides, if I had

been, I should have asked for your ladyship's strip of work."

"Give it me," cried Lady Bohun, "give it me, quick!—there, that will do—why do I stand gossipping here? Thank you."

And in another moment Lady Bohun entered the library. Sir Felix rose on her arrival. Mr. Bohun did not stir. The former gave her the chair she usually occupied on the occasions of these visits, and the latter went on with some calculations he was making, unfortunately quite unconscious of a pair of cold blue eyes fixed with unflinching steadiness on his offending head.

"Are you coming out to take a little walk, Sir Felix?" she asked.

"My dearest, it pours," was the reply.

"How provoking. Then will you come and sit in my boudoir?"

"Will you not give us the pleasure of your company here?" said Sir Felix.

Had he said "me," instead of "us," she might have complied, but the objectionable plural opened the vial of wrath.

"No thank you. If you and Mr. Bohun are engaged, I had better go back to my solitude."

This was a pleasant speech for Mr. Bohun to hear. It was intended for his special edification, and he knew it perfectly.   Mortal man could not have remained in the room after it, and the only wonder was how he kept his temper and refrained from a retort; but one look at his brother's face kept his tongue silent, and made his heart swell with sorrow instead of indignation.

"I am going," was all he answered; "the little we had to say is said and settled."

And without even a look, which could further wound his already wounded brother, he quietly left the room.

CHAPTER XVII.

WHEN two people are going to have a few words together, which they do not wish to utter before a third person, consequently, not likely to be very agreeable words, and when they only wait the exit of that third person to begin the conversation, the first few moments of the *téte-à-téte* are generally awkward ones for both parties. Neither seems quite to know how to begin. In the present case, Sir Felix courteously gave up the privilege to Lady Bohun, and certainly she was the most fitted, of the two, to commence the attack.

"Settled," said she, repeating the last word, as if it had been ringing in her ears, which indeed it had. "Settled! What have you settled, Sir Felix?"

This was opening the battle bravely; and it showed so distinctly the spirit in which she had entered the room, that Sir Felix now saw he must nerve himself for the emergency. Unfortunately, he did not feel well that day, and people out of sorts are indisposed to combat a point with much vehemence. His reply, therefore, was very mild. In few words, he explained the subjects of his conversation with his brother, and ended by saying,

"So I hope, my dearest, everything will be arranged for your comfort. That is what Guy meant by the word settled."

"But what is settled?" persisted Euphemia. "I don't see that you have altered anything. You have merely settled that things shall remain as they have been all along, and to that I do not agree. It is very fine to say 'settled,' but the person to settle things in this house is myself, Sir Felix—next to you. You seem to have settled that Mr. Bohun is to retain that room, the original boudoir?"

" I had not come to that point."

" You have settled that he is to continue to smoke at all hours under Ponsford's window?"

" My dearest, you interrupted us before I had introduced that little grievance."

" Little grievance! Do you know, Sir Felix, that if it goes on, I verily believe Ponsford will give warning?"

" Can she not change her room, Euphemia ?"

" Certainly not. Well, then, if you have not spoken to him on two out of the three requests I made you, have you broached the third?"

" You mean about Hector? Yes; I spoke about Hector, and suggested his being sent down to the kennels. Guy says if he is, he will howl in reality, and we shall be disturbed night and day. Guy suggests that we turn his kennel away from the house."

" Stuff!" cried Lady Bohun, with more emphasis than politeness; " as if that would be of the slightest use ! No, Sir Felix, the dog must go—I am quite decided about that. If you dislike saying so to Mr. Bohun, I will."

" No," interrupted her husband, hastily ; " if you wish it so much, it shall be done. I can tell Guy after luncheon. Just now I do not feel very well—my head seems to swim."

" All those stupid accounts. Why do you trouble yourself with them? Everybody else in your position has a man to do these sort of things for them."

" Guy and I have always managed Bohun Court ourselves," said Sir Felix, and Lady Bohun was silenced for the time in spite of herself.

But she was not dissatisfied with the result of

that *tête-à-tête*, small as the triumph was.   It was
a triumph all the same, and every one, however
insignificant, told in the end.

"The dog is to go, Ponsford," said she, on her
return to her room, "and that is something gained,
at all events;" and Ponsford smiled approvingly.

That day several visitors came over to Bohun
Court, and stayed to luncheon.   Euphemia liked
company, and always made herself agreeable on
these occasions, except to one or two people who
were old friends of the family, and to these she
was barely civil.   Mrs Trant was one of these, and
Mr. Melville another.

As for Mrs. Trant, she, who had always been a
sort of standing-dish in the time of all the Lady
Bohuns, her presence at the table was now a very
rare event.   The old lady was punctilious.   She did
not like, now that there was a mistress to the
house, to avail herself of the frequent invitations
of the master and his brother.   Neither did she
quite like the verbal general invitations of Lady
Bohun.   A general invitation she knew was no
invitation at all.

"People who give you general invitations, dear
Mr. Bohun," said she, one day, "never really
want you to come.   It is a polite way of keeping
you away, because, if you honestly wish to, see a

friend at dinner, it is very easy to fix a day, or even in extreme cases give a choice of days—not a general invitation. I always feel that as the greatest slight that an acquaintance can inflict upon me."

So poor old Mrs. Trant, shy and sensitive, seldom found her way to Bohun Court, and at last Sir Felix noticed it—not to the old lady, but to his wife.

Lady Bohun extricated herself from the difficulty with great ease.

"I ask her repeatedly, dear Sir Felix, but I never can get her to come. I was there only yesterday, and begged her to walk home with me and dine quietly, but she would not."

"My dearest, at her age you could not expect her to walk. We always sent the pony carriage for her."

"Well, I did not know that—how could I? I could do no more than invite her. If she cannot be induced to come, it is not my fault."

"She cannot be well. She always used to be so ready to join all our parties. But I suppose she is growing old, like the rest of us," and Sir Felix laughed.

Amongst those who sat that day at the luncheon table was Mr. Melville. As Sir Felix uttered these words, he looked up at him, and, turning to Mr. Bohun, remarked how very ill his brother was looking.

"I was noticing it this very morning," said Mr. Bohun, "and begging him to take a trip up to town for change of air and scene. He is evidently very far from well. Look how his hand shakes."

Sir Felix was pouring out a glass of wine at the moment, and could hardly do it. Euphemia, who had the faculty of hearing all that was said by everybody at table, looked at her husband, and coloured crimson.

"So!" thought she to herself, "that is what they have settled, is it?—something more than the disposal of Hector! but, I flatter myself, I can put an extinguisher on this plan at all events, if it is one of Mr. Bohun's bright ideas."

She was wary enough, however, to say nothing at the time. She waited her opportunity, for she knew Sir Felix would not take any steps without giving her some sort of notice, so she waited patiently.

"What time do you wish to drive to-day?" asked her husband, as they rose from table.

"Not to drive at all," said she, "but to take a ride with you;" and Sir Felix was so much flat-

tered by the proposal, that, ill as he felt, he gladly
entered into it.

They started at three o'clock and only returned
home in time to dress for dinner. All the afternoon Mr. Bohun had been waiting about, hoping
to waylay his brother, and impress upon him the
necessity of either change of air or medical advice.

Infinite, therefore, was his surprise when, at
dinner, Lady Bohun coolly announced that she
and Sir Felix were going up to town the following day, "for a little change."

"Oh! you go, too?" said Mr. Bohun, inad-
vertently.

"Why," exclaimed Euphemia, opening her
eyes, "you do not suppose I would let dear Sir
Felix go alone? particularly now that he is not
quite well? He has moped himself to death
here. I intend him to have a little London
gaiety, and then when I come back, I hope
mamma and some of *my* friends may come and
enliven us."

Mr. Bohun looked down, and said nothing. It
was always with some amiable little speech like this
that Lady Bohun wound up her sentences, but
he had learnt now to receive them in silence.

Still, it was impossible for him not to see, with
poignant regret, how every day revealed some

fresh trait of the craftiness and unamiability of her character.

" To what will it lead?" was always the thought uppermost in his mind, yet what but time could decide that question? There was nothing for it now but to watch, to wait, and to regret.

So Bohun Court was to be left once more to Mr. Bohun and Hector.

" By the by," said Euphemia to her husband just before they started, " you told Mr. Bohun about Hector, I suppose?"

" I quite forgot," exclaimed Sir Felix; " but, as we are going away, perhaps it will keep for another time."

" Oh! never mind now," returned Euphemia coolly, and she left the room. In the hall, as fate would have it, she met Mr. Bohun with the offender by his side.

" Mr. Bohun," said she, " Sir Felix forgot to tell you that Hector disturbs me exceedingly. I must beg that by the time I return, you will find some other place for him."

" Certainly," replied her brother-in-law, " the kennels......."

" Anywhere, out of hearing," retorted Lady Bohun, pointedly, and went on her way.

So disagreeable was the impression made upon
Mr. Bohun by these words, and the tone in which
they were delivered, that they haunted him all
day. Like a restless spirit, when the confusion
of the departure was over, did he wander through
all the deserted rooms, the dog by his side, and
think sadly over the days gone by, when Bohun
Court was to him what it never could be again.

He entered, at last, Lady Bohun's boudoir, a
room he had scarcely seen, for she had never invited him in, and seemed purposely to avoid doing
so, but now the door stood wide open, and he
paused and gazed round.

How altered! how perfectly different to what
it once had been! Not a vestige of the old furniture left—not even a tint on the walls the same.
Everything was white, and gold, and gay colouring. The carpet dark, rich, and with a broad
border of rather gaudy colours; the curtains to
match, and a heavy but handsome *portière* hiding
the doors which communicated with the dining-
room, and recently put up to intercept the draught
of which Lady Bohun had once complained.

Then, on the tables and scattered about, were
such a multiplicity of little fancy objects, bearing
Paris on their faces; statuettes on brackets, vases
of Bohemian glass, cups and tazzas of Sèvres

china, books, paper-knives, inkstands, and work
baskets; all, in short, heaped together in beautiful confusion.

Then the chairs and sofas! No wonder her
dainty ladyship so seldom graced the drawing-
room with her presence; in this, her own peculiar
room, was a chair or a sofa for every hour of the
day, and every frame of her fitful mind, and
about a dozen cushions of every form and device
under the sun.

"No," thought he to himself, "I never should
have known the room again;" and as he still continued to gaze, the heavy *portière* was suddenly
put aside, and a figure stood before him—Ponsford—the vampire!

A graceful start, and a shrinking back, and
then a sliding advance, marked her recognition of
his presence, and then, with her usual patronizing
gentleness, she exclaimed,

"Oh! Mr. Bohun, don't let me disturb you,
sir" (he had evinced no intention of being disturbed, but had walked into the recess of the
window, and was looking out), "I am just putting away a few of her ladyship's things."

"Do you not accompany Lady Bohun, then?"
asked Mr. Bohun, surprised to see her there.

"I *follow* her ladyship, sir," was the reply,

uttered with a sort of dignified affability, "but I could not leave before I had put away a few of her ladyship's particular favourites which might be injured by exposure to the air; besides, I have to lock up these rooms; but," she added, "there is no hurry, sir—pray do not go on my account."

Mr. Bohun could hardly conceal a smile at the idea of being permitted by Ponsford to remain in the room! However, he said nothing; but stood quietly in the window, and watched her as she glided about. He amused himself thus for several minutes, till at last he saw that he was himself being watched by her! that instead of putting away, and locking up, she flitted from table to table, and chair to chair, and did nothing! evidently, on the contrary (and ostentatiously), waiting for him to go.

And with inward disgust and contempt he at last did go, and angrily shut himself up in his den.

"That woman infuriates me with myself," thought he, as he threw himself into his chair; "she rouses in me all sorts of ill feeling, malice, and hatred, which would otherwise remain dormant in my composition. Thank goodness, in two hours the house will be rid of her."

Yes, in two hours, for a glance at a Bradshaw

had shown him that in two hours the last train
that day would start—"and in two hours,"
thought he, "she cannot do much harm, luckily."

But in direful contradiction of this comfortable
self-assurance, there came in one short hour afterwards, a sharp, quick knock at Mr. Bohun's door,
and at his rather startled permission to "Come
in," the figure of the trim little old housekeeper
instantly presented itself.

A patch of colour, like paint, was on each
cheekbone of Mrs. Dance's usually pale and placid
face, and her hands trembled nervously, as she
vainly endeavoured to keep her fingers decorously
interlaced.

"May I make bold, sir," she began, "to say a
few words to you?"

Mr. Bohun laughed.

"Why, Dance, I suppose if you wish it, you
must; but I confess I always dread 'a few words,'
just as a burnt child......you know the rest."

"Ah! sir, I am truly sorry, and I don't wonder at your dreading it, for I am sure I know
what it is to dread just as you do, sir; but things
cannot go on as they do, sir, and now they have
come to a pitch that really obliges me to speak to
you."

"Well, Dance, say on then, but you must at

the same time bear in mind how scrupulously I have for months past abstained from the slightest interference, direct or indirect, with the affairs of this household."

"True, sir; but in the absence of Sir Felix, this is a case in which I hope you will see fit to interfere. Mrs. Ponsford, not satisfied with locking up the reception rooms, so that if you had friends to dinner you would not have a room to sit in but this, has also asked for the keys of the store-room, and declares that my lady ordered her to lock that up too!"

Mr. Bohun was silent and perplexed. "This seems strange," was all he could say.

"But is it to be allowed, sir?" asked the old housekeeper, hastily. "Am I to give them up? because Mrs. Ponsford is waiting for them."

"By Lady Bohun's orders?"

"So she says, sir."

"Then give them up, Dance."

The old woman paused a moment. "You desire it, sir?" said she.

"Not I, I have nothing to do with it. You ask my advice, apparently, not my orders—for those I am not empowered or disposed to give; but my advice is, comply quietly with the commands left by Lady Bohun."

"Then, sir," said the little housekeeper, drawing up the trim figure; "may I humbly beg you to......to let me resign my place here......the situation must be filled by some one else......I am not the person to suit my lady......I saw your good father and mother married, and Sir Felix and yourself christened, Mr. Guy, and I did hope to live and serve you to the last, but it can't be done, sir......I have tried my utmost and it can't be done. I humbly beg to give warning, sir...... for the first time in my life......and if you will please to break it to Sir Felix......"

Vexed beyond concealment, yet nearly betrayed into a smile by the last expression, Mr. Bohun now instantly put an extinguisher on the conversation.

"No, Dance," said he, "that you must do yourself. I hope, on reflection, you will see how very foolish it will be of you to do any such thing, but if you persist, the act must be your own. As for me, you are in my eyes so completely part and parcel of Bohun Court, that I should as soon think of the old house itself marching, as of your leaving it. However, with that I have nothing to do, and let me know nothing about it. I believe the best advice I can give you is, to obey the ruling powers."

"It is very hard at my time of life," sobbed the old woman; "and very bitter to have a young woman like that set over one's head."

"We have all our trials and troubles," returned Mr. Bohun; "I remember my mother used to say everybody had something to bear for somebody else's sake."

"Yes, Mr. Guy, but then you care for them. It is hard to suffer for a thankless person. I would bear anything in the world for the sake of you or Sir Felix, but for Mrs. Ponsford!......"

Mr. Bohun began to walk up and down the room in silence—the old lady took the silence as a hint for her absence—and the interview closed; but, as she left the room, Mr. Bohun instinctively glanced at the clock—one hour only remained— "in an hour the house will be free of her"—and he drew a long breath.

But again the door opens. The tall, portly old butler appears.

"If you please, sir, William wants to speak to you."

William was one of the stable men, and a doubtful adherent of the family. People said he was rather won over by the honeyed words of Mrs. Ponsford, for whom he often rode on errands to the adjacent town. He did not belong particularly to either Sir Felix or Mr. Bohun, but was a sort of supernumerary, and did work for all parties.

He came in shamefaced, rather red, and not looking Mr. Bohun straight in the face. Hector, lying on the rug, gave a low growl like distant thunder, as he entered.

"What is it?" asked Mr. Bohun, almost inclined to say, "What is it, *now?*"

"If you please, sir......I'm to drive Mrs. Ponsford to the station."

"Well?" with an impatient jerk of the head.

"And please, sir, shall I take Hector down to the kennels first?"

Mr. Bohun looked as if he did not understand.

"Hector, down to the kennels? What do you mean?"

"Mrs. Ponsford, sir......"

Mr. Bohun's eyes glared, and he forgot himself.

"What the devil have either you or Mrs. Ponsford to do with taking Hector down to the kennels?"

The man grew redder still.

"Beg pardon, sir, but Mrs. Ponsford said her orders was, not to leave the house till the dog was......was......"

"Was what?"

"Disposed of, sir, was her words."

And now Mr. Bohun set his teeth very hard. If he had a weak point in the world, it was Hector. About Hector he was as foolish as a child, and to think that this woman, whose rule was now spreading all over the house, should presume to extend her influence beyond it, and dictate to the out-door servants, was beyond endurance. No! Perhaps Hector should go to the kennels, but not now; not at that woman's bidding.

"Leave the room," said Mr. Bohun, neither calmy nor temperately; "leave the room, and the next time you dare to enter my presence on such an errand, is your last hour in the service of Sir Felix Bohun. Leave the room, and let me caution you to beware. Down! Hector."

The dog had risen; he stood close by his master's side, the corners of his mouth hanging down, his eyes gleaming with the red light which always gave them their fearful expression when their owner was displeased; he kept looking alternately from master to man, as if asking permission to be allowed to dart forward and strangle the latter, since his instinct told him that he and the former were falling out, and his affection prompted expeditious punishment. But the "Down!

Hector," restrained the hot blood, and on the man's speedy retreat, the dog returned to his rug, and his master to his walk up and down the room.

As he did so, the words of Miss Maynard, spoken in one of her wild, careless moods recurred to him.

" Yes," thought he, " the poison has begun to work; the vampire has begun at her deadly trade, sucking away comfort, peace, and happiness! Miss Maynard was right."

Suddenly—a draught of air in the room—he stopped, started—there she · stood before him, calm, pale, and with a face which looked like a Parian lamp with the light shining behind it. There was something so singular in this transparency of Ponsford's complexion that no one who ever saw her could fail to be struck with it.

Mr. Bohun stood, struck dumb at her effrontery.

"I beg your pardon, Mr. Bohun," said she, with a smile—a smile, to re-assure him!—" but I thought you said ' Come in?'"

" I am not aware that you knocked at all at my door," replied Mr. Bohun, in a tone which would have daunted any one else.

" Indeed, I did, sir; but the fact is, my train

obliges me to be abrupt—so you will forgive the intrusion, I hope. Her ladyship left several orders with me which, I believe, I have now executed, all excepting one—your dog, excuse me, sir—did I understand rightly from William? Her ladyship left orders with me to see that it was removed before her return—that means, of course, *removed to-day*, otherwise I could not personally superintend......"

"Mrs. Ponsford," broke in Mr. Bohun, "I cannot believe that the orders you received from Lady Bohun could possibly extend to matters quite beyond your jurisdiction. Confine yourself, if you please, to affairs over which you have a right to exercise authority—not to mine, I beg."

Another smile, soft and pitying. "Her ladyship, sir, so distinctly mentioned the dog, and expressed such an unmistakable wish—an order, in fact—that she should not find it within hearing on her return, in short, that I should see, myself, that it was conveyed to a distance entirely out of hearing, that unless I decidedly fail in gaining your permission, I must see the orders carried into effect."

"You have failed," was Mr. Bohun's reply.

Her eyes met his. His quailed, not hers!

"Am I at liberty to tell her ladyship this?"

she asked, still gently, for Ponsford never raised
her voice, never got excited, never looked angry.
On occasions when most eyes sparkle or flash
fire, she prudently veiled hers with those large
white lids.

"Pray say what you please," said he. She
made him a curtsey which a *débutante* at Court
might have envied, and wishing him good afternoon, in her usual voice, left the room.

Mr. Bohun glanced again at the clock, and saw
it wanted half an hour of the time.

"It will take her that to get to the station.
She will miss the train, by Jove!"

And he grew uneasy, pacing the room with
hurried step and a quivering lip, feeling, to the
tips of his fingers, how, under a semblance of
perfect civility, a menial had that day found
means to insult and infuriate him.

"Will she miss the train?" he again thought;
and again the very minutes were counted. If she
missed it, she would return to Bohun Court—
sleep under the same roof as himself—exhale,
like the upas, her poison throughout the atmosphere
he breathed.

But, hush! Wheels driving round his side of
the house. Wheels—a pause—and wheels again.
She was off; but, perhaps, not gone. She might

miss the train; and Mr. Bohun deliberately sat
down in his chair by the window, and, moreover,
sat there one whole hour, determined to watch
for the return of the pony chaise. From his
window he could see it pass behind a narrow belt
of young trees, to the stables. He could see if
the stable-helper, appointed to drive her, returned
alone or not.

In an hour he returned, and alone.

"Then she is fairly off," and Mr. Bohun got
up and breathed again. "Come, Hector!" said
he, "stir up, old dog. Come, and let us shake
off the ugly mood that is on us. We have gone
through troubles hitherto unknown to-day, Hector,
and we have made two enemies. We have got to
fight the world now, Hector, and our way does
not lie smooth before us. Stir up briskly, my
old friend, and let us face our worries in the
open air. It blows away many a grievance. But
we have got a skeleton in our house, and you and
I must face it. Let us take a walk together,
and think over what we can do."

"William," said the old coachman to the helper
that evening, "didn't I hear as how Hector was
to be took down to the kennels to-night? Wasn't
you to fetch him?"

" So Mrs. Ponsford said; and I went to Mr. Bohun, and he was mortal angry and dared me to."

" Then, in course, he ain't going, and you may take down that young setter of Sir Felix's, and put him in the big kennel instead."

" But didn't I ought to take Hector, too?"

": When Mr. Bohun told you not?"

" But Mrs. Ponsford said particklar......"

" Mrs. Ponsford be ——. If you go minding Mrs. Ponsford against Mr. Bohun, I'll make the place too hot to hold you.   Be off with you!"

CHAPTER XVIII.

THEY went away for two or three days: they remained away two months; and all that time Mr. Bohun was locked out of every room in Bohun Court, except the two appropriated to himself, and the large, dull, cheerless dining-room, which he never entered. He could certainly have invited four-and-twenty friends to dine with him, had he chosen it, but he could not have asked one to stay all night. Not a bedroom was left open. Mrs. Dance announced the fact with a flood of tears, and Mr. Bohun heard it with the composure of a stoic.

But he had made up his mind to all this. Nothing surprised him now; but there was stirring within him by this time a resolution which solitude would give him firmness to put into execution. It was, no longer to reside beneath the roof that had been his home so long; and this absence of

Sir Felix was the most opportune circumstance
that could have befallen him, as far as his plan
was concerned, since as long as his brother was
present, he actually had not the heart to resist
his entreaties that he would remain.

But now his mind was made up. The system
of persecution, insult, and impertinence, all veiled
under a specious garb, was no longer to be en-
dured, and the opportunity for releasing himself
had arrived.

" Mrs. Trant was right," he used often to say,
as he mused by himself; " I ought never to have
subjected myself to this life. I ought to have
retired with dignity a year ago, just as Mrs. Dance
has been wishing to do every month of her life
under the new reign; but I was a fool, and treated
Mrs. Trant's hints and innuendos with carelessness
—consequently, my punishment has overtaken
me. But it is over now. It is not compulsory
that I should live with a skeleton in my cupboard;
henceforth I will have a cupboard to myself."
And armed with this resolution, he put on his hat,
took Hector by the ear, and prepared to walk
down to Mrs. Trant's cottage, and communicate
it to her.

It had been so long the custom of the Bohuns
to tell Mrs. Trant all their thoughts, actions, and

intentions, that he did this as a matter of course; but, as he took his way through the plantations, in crossing the high road, he encountered Mr. Melville, and then recollected that he had not seen him for several days.

" My dear friend, what have you been doing with yourself?"

" I have been in town," said the old clergyman, "and was summoned up on business so hastily, that I had not time to ask if you had any commands. But I saw Sir Felix."

" Did you?" replied Mr. Bohun; " I dare say I shall see him myself before long, for I have some idea of going up in a day or two."

" I am glad of it," returned Mr. Melville, so pointedly that Mr. Bohun's keen eyes fixed themselves rather steadily on him; " I am glad of it, because I saw no prospect of their coming down here, though a London life evidently does not agree with Sir Felix."

Now Mr. Bohun and his brother were in frequent, nay, constant correspondence with each other. Not three days passed without the interchange of letters, and the former was aware that Sir Felix had not derived that benefit from the change which he had expected, nor which the scraps invariably added by Lady Bohun to the

letters, wished to lead him to infer. But this
kind of correspondence was not satisfactory. It
was not the voluntary outpourings of an unwatched
pen. It was epistolization under the restraint of
continual supervision.

The letters were not those of Sir Felix. They
all bore traces of Lady Bohun. Consequently,
Mr. Bohun never felt sure that he had the right
version of either his brother's health or anything
else, and was quite ready to take alarm when his
old friend professed himself glad to hear that he
was going up to town.

" Then, my brother was not looking well?"
was his first question.

" Very far from well, and out of spirits."

" Is it possible? Lady Bohun describes their
life as a whirl of gaiety."

" Lady Bohun goes out a great deal, I believe:
but not Sir Felix: that is, not when he can help
it. I was to have dined with him one day *téte-à
téte*, Lady Bohun being engaged to go out to her
father's near London, but on her return home
from her afternoon's drive, she positively insisted
on his accompanying her, and made me a great
many very polite apologies, begging me to fix
another day, which, however, I was unable to do."

How like her was even this little circumstance!

how like the jealousy which marked every action of her life! but Mr. Melville did not appear to have seen it in this light. To him it only seemed a little piece of tyranny, strongly savouring of selfishness.

"I was in hopes," began Mr. Bohun again, "that they would soon be thinking of home. Bohun Court looks so beautiful just now."

"Ah! my dear Mr. Bohun, the young lady sees more beauty in London at the present season, I fancy, and Sir Felix is under advice."

"That makes me uneasy. My brother has hardly ever had a doctor in his life. Does he look ill?"

"There is a look about him I do not like."

"So there was before he left home."

"True; and it has gained upon him. He is not what he was; but as, perhaps, you know, he suffers from a numbness in the limbs, and I had hardly a moment alone with him, owing to the presence of a servant, who was rubbing his feet during the greater part of my visit."

"This is something quite new to me," exclaimed Mr. Bohun, anxiously. "Neither my brother nor Lady Bohun have ever hinted at such a thing. A numbness? Good Heavens! that looks like paralysis!"

"Let us hope not; but, as I told you, I had no opportunity to speak privately with him as to his health."

"Owing to the presence of the man-servant?"

"Not a man, my dear friend—Lady Bohun's own maid—apparently, a very valuable servant, who never leaves him when her mistress is out."

"Ponsford, by Jove!" almost burst from Mr. Bohun's lips, but, drawing them in tightly, he refrained. Ponsford, the vampire! the skeleton in the cupboard! Ponsford mounting guard over the invalid to the exclusion of his friends!

"A villainous plot, to gain some end at present a mystery," thought Mr. Bohun, and hastily bidding his friend adieu, he pursued his way to Mrs. Trant's, determined that two days more should find him by his brother's side—and no Ponsford to play third hand.

"You are right," said Mrs. Trant, when after an hour's conversation she had learnt all his plans; "you have come to a right decision, and I only wish you could have arrived at it before your reluctance to disoblige Sir Felix had brought down so much annoyance upon you. But the oldest of us sometimes have to learn by experience, and you have bought yours dearly. When do you go?"

"I shall go to-morrow. I was in no haste until I met Mr. Melville, but now I am uneasy; uneasy at his account of my brother's health, and uneasy at the ignorance in which I have been kept. Fortunately, I am not sufficiently afraid of Lady Bohun to hesitate to demand the reason of so much concealment. All the petty annoyances to which I have been subjected appear trifles in my sight now in comparison with this. Who has a better right to know of my brother's indisposition than myself?"

"His wife," said Mrs. Trant, quietly; "take care how you encroach on what she considers her property and prerogative. Unless I am much mistaken, she will submit to no interference where Sir Felix is concerned."

"Despicable jealousy!" exclaimed Mr. Bohun, getting up, and walking about the room.

"Wives don't like family interference," persisted the old lady.

"Can she call my affection and interest interference?" asked Mr. Bohun.

"Go up to town and see," was the reply, "and when you come back tell me who is right; but be temperate, dear Mr. Guy! Do you know, that I almost think mature age is bringing sourness to your spirit?"

· " It is !" he exclaimed, heartily; "as ever, you
are right. I *am* soured! soured by reading a
most unamiable page of life, and rendered bitter
by becoming acquainted with human nature in an
unpleasant form. I acknowledge it with regret;
but my temper is being spoilt. Mrs. Trant, it is
high time that I should live alone again. It does
not do to try and make a family man of an old
bachelor."

" I say nothing to that," said Mrs. Trant, " but
to your having a roof of your own I cordially
assent. As to your temper, few people live to
your time of life having had so little to try them.
The consequence is, when you are tried, you are
found wanting."

" I like your truths, dear old friend," was Mr.
Bohun's frank rejoinder, as he prepared to take
his leave, "and I will endeavour to do my best to
keep the peace during my sojourn in town; but
I go prepared for a struggle—a struggle with
both Sir Felix and my lady; the one will try to
hold me fast, the other will do her utmost to
shake me off."

" And she will succeed," said Mrs. Trant.

" I know it," was the answer; and the next
day Mr. Bohun went up to town.

Sir Felix had taken a house for the season, in

a fashionable square. When Mr. Bohun, in a cab, drove up to the door, two footmen, strangers to him, were lounging at the door, and Lady Bohun's carriage was waiting at a little distance.

"Is Sir Felix at home?" he asked, instinctively.

"Not at home, sir," came immediately.

"I shall come in all the same," said Mr. Bohun, coolly, "and be so good as to bring in my bag."

"Who can it be?" whispered one man to the other, and by this time Mr. Bohun was in the hall. Hardly had he advanced to the dining-room door than it opened, and he met Lady Bohun face to face.

"Good gracious, Mr. Bohun! how you startled me!"

"How is my brother, Lady Bohun?"

"Sir Felix! Oh! dear, very well, thank you, that is, pretty well considering; but don't stand here in the hall. Come up into the drawing-room."

"My brother is out, I hear."

"Did they say, not at home? Ah! that was because we were just going out to take a drive. Come up, Mr. Bohun," and he followed her into the drawing-room expecting to find Sir Felix there; but no such thing.

·"Sit down, Mr. Bohun; pretty house, is it not? and when did you come up to town?"

"I have this moment arrived."

"London is very full. It will bewilder you after Bohun Court."

"If Felix is at home, will you be kind enough to say in what room I shall find him, for I do not like detaining you from your drive."

"Oh! we were both going out. We always hunt in couples; but you wait here a moment, and I will go and tell him."

Taken off his guard, Mr. Bohun suffered himself to be left in the drawing-room, and Lady Bohun went forthwith up to her room—not down to Sir Felix. "Ponsford," said she, in a breathless whisper, "Mr. Bohun has arrived. Now, listen; go down and rub Sir Felix till I come and release you. Then get ready the spare beds for mamma and Fanny Washington. I shall drive out to The Laurels, and bring them both back, and Mr. Aylmer with them; so get all the spare rooms ready. I am not going to have Mr. Bohun *here*. You understand—not another bed by any possibility to be made up; and if, by chance, I have to go without Sir Felix, don't you leave him if you can help it."

"And if I cannot help it, my lady?"

" Why, then, manage the best way you can. No private conversations, you know."

" No, my lady."

And away flew Euphemia, having scarcely left Mr. Bohun five minutes.

She found him pacing the drawing-room impatiently, and saw at a glance that his ire was rising.

" Now come and see Sir Felix," said she, with a cheerfulness which irritated him still more. " He seldom honours this room—he prefers a luxurious little boudoir that we have downstairs."

" I am sorry you thought it necessary to take the trouble of preparing him to see *me*," said Mr. Bohun, following her moodily ; " I hope his state of health requires no such precaution as *that*."

" Oh, dear no !"—and she tripped lightly down before him—" on the contrary, your arrival will be a charming surprise to him ; only you know he has not been very strong for some weeks past, so I generally announce any little pieces of news to him myself, for fear of his being startled. Not that I have done so on the present occasion ; I have only ascertained that he is not taking a nap, which he sometimes does after a fit of pain. This is his room," and Mr. Bohun suddenly found himself behind the chair of his brother, who, unaware of his entrance, was submitting to having his feet rubbed by an individual whose lambent eyes gleamed full upon Mr. Bohun, as he stood there, uncertain and perplexed.

"Dear Sir Felix, how is the pain?" asked the honeyed tongue.

"Oh, my dearest! really quite well. I have been assuring Ponsford so, only I cannot induce her to believe me. I feel perfectly able to walk to the carriage. Did you say I was to drive, Ponsford?"

"Oh, yes! Sir Felix, if you please."

"But first, dear Sir Felix, I have such a pleasant surprise for you. I have brought you a visitor," said Euphemia.

"Oh, Euphemia! I really cannot talk to Mr. Aylmer again to-day. His spirits are so over-powering."

"Not Mr. Aylmer — somebody else;" and, standing on one side, Lady Bohun held out her hand to Mr. Bohun, who, an amazed spectator of a scene which made his brother appear in the light of a person in a state of imbecility, had stood mute, until now brought forward.

The change in the countenance of Sir Felix, when he saw his brother, was something marvellous. It was as if light irradiated every feature; and though his feet were apparently held fast by Ponsford, he turned himself in his chair, and held out both his hands, with a gesture of delighted astonishment.

"Of all people in the world, my good Guy! Why, this is new life to me! When did you come, and what powerful motive, stronger than all my entreaties, has brought you up?"

"Have you ever entreated me? Surely not? If you had, I should have been here before."

"Entreated you in every letter. Euphemia is my witness, as well as my amanuensis; these flying pains have made my hands very helpless lately, but she has repeatedly tried to tempt you up." Mr. Bohun glanced at Lady Bohun, but she was tying on her veil at the glass. "However, now I have got you here, Guy, I shall not let you go in a hurry—here, sit down. Thank you, Ponsford, I will not trouble you any longer. Euphemia, my dear, you will excuse my accompanying you to-day."

"Oh, dear Sir Felix! Mr. Bohun will not permit you to lose your drive, I am sure."

"Then he must go with us. Guy, where is your luggage? have they taken it up stairs? Ponsford, will you be good enough to see it taken to Mr. Bohun's room?"

Ponsford looked pleadingly from Sir Felix to Lady Bohun, and then back again.

"The rooms, Sir Felix......unfortunately...... the rooms are every one full.".

"Yes, dear Sir Felix, how very unlucky! Don't you recollect? Mamma, and Miss Washington, and Mr. Aylmer—don't you remember? —we engaged to go and bring them all here to-day."

"I don't recollect a word about it," exclaimed Sir Felix; "but, at all events, a room must be found."

"Not to put you to inconvenience," began Mr. Bohun, fixing his eyes on Lady Bohun.

"Pshaw, my dear fellow! inconvenience in a house that makes up two-and-twenty beds?"

"Mamma shall be put off, if you wish it," said Lady Bohun; "I dare say she will not much mind."

"Not for the world," returned her brother-in-law; "for, to tell you the truth, my arrangements are all made. But now about yourself, Felix. I was not prepared to find you an invalid. How is it you never told me of your illness? Have you *had* an illness?"

"He has been ailing a little—nothing very serious, I am thankful to say," said Lady Bohun, patting Sir Felix on the head like a child; "and hoping that every day would bring an amendment, we have not liked to make you uneasy, Mr. Bohun, knowing your anxious temperament."

Mr. Bohun had never heard of this ingredient in his composition before, and no one possessed of less perfect self-control and equanimity would have borne it so well. As it was, nothing but that peculiar pinch about his mouth betrayed what was passing within his mind.

"Who is your medical man?" was his next question.

"Dr. J——, a most able, eminent man," said Lady Bohun.

"The greatest ruffian I ever encountered," exclaimed Sir Felix in the same breath; "so much so, that I begged Mrs. Blackstone never to bring the fellow here again."

"Not a doctor of your own selection, then," said his brother, boldly.

"Dear Sir Felix," interrupted his wife, before he could reply, "Mr. Bohun will forgive me, but indeed the beauty of the day is passing. We shall see him at dinner, of course, but I am sure he will join his entreaties to mine that you should take your usual drive."

Mr. Bohun never uttered a syllable.

"Usual drive?" echoed the invalid, fractiously; "good heavens! haven't I been tied to this chair since......"

Lady Bohun and Ponsford exchanged lightning glances, and before the sentence could be finished, the latter said very calmly, but rapidly—

"Dr. J—— was to come to-day, at three, Sir Felix, and it only wants ten minutes."

Up started the victim. "Then, my dear Guy, good-bye till dinner, for I'll cheat the fellow. Here, give me your arm—forgive me, Guy, but I cannot stand that man—no one else could have induced me to leave you, but be sure I find you here when I come home. I have volumes to talk to you about, and I only grieve that you are not to be under this roof—my home and your's should always be one."

And chattering on, with his arm through Mr. Bohun's and his hand on his wife's shoulder, Sir Felix passed through the hall, tottering, feeble, and infirm—was almost lifted into the carriage—and, waving his hand to his brother, was speedily driven out of sight, whilst Mr. Bohun stood on the steps, and heard the ostentatious order of Lady Bohun given, "to The Laurels."

CHAPTER XIX.

MR. BOHUN turned on the step and re-entered the house, absently retracing his steps to the room in which he had had this interview with his brother.

"I may as well wait till this doctor comes, and learn the truth at once," mused he. "It wants but a quarter of an hour to the time. I will wait."

And he sat down lost in thought. He had had a shock, and he wanted time to rally from it. It was a shock to have seen Sir Felix in that state. Two months had done the work of two years; and, to Mr. Bohun's eyes, his brother seemed either recovering from, or on the verge of, a stroke of paralysis—not only paralysis of the limbs, but extending to the brain, for surely no one, in his rational or reasonable senses, would submit to such coaxing and cajoling as that to which he had just been an astonished and disgusted witness.

There had been a wide march in the manner of both Lady Bohun and Ponsford towards Sir Felix since Mr. Bohun had last seen them all together. The manner of the former was coaxing and fawning, as though for some hidden purpose; the manner of the latter a sort of smiling, but determined command, as though she knew and felt her power over him. At Bohun Court there was nothing like this. Neither would have dared in those days, (and yet how few the days were ago,) to have assumed such a tone towards Sir Felix Bohun !

" He has had a stroke, or a touch very nearly approaching it, and for their own purposes I have been kept in ignorance," mused Mr. Bohun; " but I will not be baffled; I will wait and see the doctor, and fathom the truth before I leave the house, and this evening, alone with Felix, I shall be able to judge to what extent the mischief or the malady has gone."

To Mr. Bohun it had at first seemed very sudden, this complete change in his brother, but now that he came to think it over, he recollected how ailing he had been during the early months of the year—how often depressed and out of spirits—

how often looking ill without any positive complaint.

"And I passed it all by, thinking Felix never could be ill."

Such was the sort of reproach with which all Mr. Bohun's mental cogitations ended.

"But *they* saw he was ill," he continued to himself; "they saw and knew more than I, and took their measures accordingly, blinding me at the time, blinding me to the last, and wishing to blind me even now, in defiance of the evidence of my own senses. But never mind. To-night, alone with him, I shall come at the true state of things, and a few words with his doctor will set me all right."

And again looking at the clock he saw the hands on the stroke of three.

Medical men are punctual. Mr. Bohun, therefore, was not impatient, but he was not suffered to remain long in solitary expectation. The old butler had only heard of his arrival as the carriage drove away, but instantly arming himself with a tray of wine and biscuits, he hurried up as fast as his ancient legs could carry him, and bustling into the room, poured out his congratulations simultaneously with the best sherry the cellars boasted.

His greetings occupied but few sentences; the subject uppermost in his mind was the same which engrossed Mr. Bohun.

"Dear heart, sir, did you ever see such a change as in Sir Felix!" uttered more as an exclamation admitting of no doubt, than as a question.

"Burley, I am shocked," was all Mr. Bohun answered.

"I knew you would be, sir. I've had more than half a mind for many a day to make bold and write you a letter, and tell you how things was going on, and how Sir Felix was failing like, and how he was worretted and fidgetted, what with the doctors, and the friends, and the relations, and the strange gentlemen what I takes to be......" the old man sunk his voice to a whisper, and backing to the door, closed it; "what I takes to be lawyers, though, thinks I, Sir Felix isn't fit for business, and it's Mr. Bohun as should come and do it for him, and says I, every day to myself, I'll make free and write."

"Oh, why did you not?" exclaimed Mr. Bohun, whose countenance had assumed a new and startled expression during the delivery of this sentence; "I knew nothing of all this! You should indeed have written."

"I would, sir, but how could I, when day after day I hears my lady promise to do it, and I puts her letters in the post myself to make sure you should get them, and every day I thinks to myself, he'll come to-day, sure enough, but no!"

"Many a letter have I had, but not one to bid me come to town," said Mr. Bohun, and then he was sorry he had said so much, for old Burley caught at the words.

"You don't mean it, sir! bless you, then you don't know half we've gone through. Oh! sir, Mrs. Ponsford......she's at the bottom of everything. She rules Sir Felix, and my lady daren't say her soul's her own for her, though I don't believe my lady feels it as Sir Felix does. My lady thinks all Mrs. Ponsford says and does is perfection, but poor master......"

The old man sighed, and Mr. Bohun, afraid to trust himself to speak, merely looked interrogatively at him.

"Poor master tried hard for his own way, at first, sir, but he had such a lot about him."

"How do you mean, a lot?"

"All my lady's......but, sir, I'd better hold my tongue......you'll see, you'll see, sir. Of course, you stay in the house, sir?"

"No, Burley. I prefer my own rooms where

I always go in town. I'm growing old enough to like independence."

"Oh! sir, it's a blessed word! a word we don't know much of *here*."

"But it is the health of my brother that causes me most anxiety," said Mr. Bohun. "I do not like to see him in this state, Burley. How long has he been so?"

"Only really bad this last three weeks, sir."

"Three weeks! Good heavens! so long! Was he taken suddenly ill?"

"Can't say, sir. Everything up stairs is kept so snug, only I notices little things. There was two bottles of brandy went up one day in particular, and the new doctor came, what Mrs. Washington brought."

"Who is Mrs. Washington?"

"My lady's great friend, sir."

"By the by, why does not the doctor arrive? I am waiting for him. He was to be here at three."

"Was he, sir?"

"Was he not?"

"Not to my knowledge, sir."

"Ponsford said so."

"Did she, sir? Then perhaps she said so to make Sir Felix go out. I've heard her do it before; it was one day that Mr. Melville was calling, sir, and poor master wanted to stay at home and have a talk with him, only my lady said he must take his drive for his health, and he is so mortal afraid of that doctor, sir, that he'd run—even from you, sir!—to get out of seeing him."

Mr. Bohun could put "two and two together," as well as anybody else. This conversation enlightened him on several points; and seeing now that to wait for an individual who was evidently not coming, or expected, would be rather like a loss of time, he turned towards the door, and ordered a cab to convey him to his own quarters.

He was no longer in a humour to talk. He could not have talked any longer, even on the subject nearest his heart, so full was it now of grief, vexation, and perplexity.

He saw the plot that was laid, and the game that was being played. The same power which had prevented a *tête-à-tête* between Sir Felix and his old friend Mr. Melville, had that day been successfully exerted to prevent any private conversation between the brothers.

"The skeleton is in full play," thought Mr. Bohun; "there must be something they wish to conceal; something they are afraid of;" but his nature was far too unsuspicious to imagine what it could be.

He looked forward, however, to the evening to unravel the mystery. Between himself and Sir Felix there had never, as yet, been any secrets. Alone together after dinner, when Lady Bohun and her mother and her friend should have left the table, he depended upon learning all that he wished to know. Perhaps, even if he went half-an-hour before dinner-time, he could steal a few moments then; so he started early, and had the satisfaction of having the door opened by a foot-man with a frown on his face, and only one arm in his coat sleeve. His early appearance was evi-dently looked upon as an unwarrantable liberty.

In the drawing-room a similar reception awaited him. The housemaid was smoothing down the furniture, and putting the chairs and tables in their places.

" Has Sir Felix returned from his drive?" he asked.

" Yes, sir," said the well-known voice of the vampire, at his elbow, " some time ago. Sir Felix felt a little fatigued, and is resting on the sofa in her ladyship's room."

In safe custody evidently; so Mr. Bohun sat down and took up a book till the rustling of silks and satins, like the wings of a flight of birds, warned him it was seven o'clock, and time to begin to play company.

"This is mamma, Mr. Bohun, whom you remember, I dare say, and Mrs. Washington, who says she had the pleasure of sitting next you at our wedding breakfast. I am sorry to say, my friend Fanny could not come; but......" and at this moment Sir Felix tottered in, held in the vigorous grasp of a fair young man with pendent whiskers and moustaches......"allow me to introduce my cousin, Sydney Aylmer."

The young man, whose spirits Sir Felix had only that afternoon so piteously declared were too much for him! A case of the spider and the fly. Sir Felix seemed to writhe in the grasp which had fastened on him, and appeared not to intend to let him go until it had deposited its burden in a chair.

"There you are, Sir Felix, safe and sound. Mr. Bohun, I am delighted to make your acquaintance. Come, cheer up, Sir Felix, you look quite yourself again to-day."

"Thank you, Mr. Aylmer, you are very good, and I know you mean to be very kind; but if I could only convince you how much better I could get on if you would be so obliging as to let me walk unassisted......"

"My dear Sir Felix, you know it keeps Lady Bohun in a constant state of alarm and anxiety, so you really must submit to my attentions. It is no trouble. I am charmed to be of use. What are looking for?"

"Nothing, thank you, Mr. Aylmer."

"I am sure you were. Tell me, and let me find it. Have you dropped your handkerchief? Shall I go and ask for it?"

Sir Felix leant back in his chair, silent.

"You feel faint—here are Phemy's salts."

Sir Felix had the greatest objection to any one calling Lady Bohun by her Christian name, even a cousin.

"I thank you, Mr. Aylmer, but Lady Bohun herself would never venture to offer me salts. I have a horror of them. My dear Guy, come and take a chair by me. I have hardly seen you. The long drive quite knocked me up, so Lady Bohun insisted on my resting in her room, other-wise I quite reckoned on a chat with you; how-ever......"

"Dinner, Sir Felix," said the sonorous voice of the old butler, and instantly the procession formed.

"Sydney," whispered Lady Bohun, as they went down stairs, "don't you leave Sir Felix alone with Mr. Bohun after dinner. He will talk him to death."

The consequence was, that Mr. Aylmer remained a fixture in the dining-room until, worn to a thread-paper by his ceaseless conversation, vapid and frivolous, yet vociferously demanding attention, Sir Felix begged his brother to assist him upstairs, and gave up all idea of a *tête-à-tête* as a hopeless case.

At last, Mr. Bohun managed to edge in a word *sotto voce.*

" Felix, who is that young man ?"

" A standing-dish, of which I would give anybody fifty pounds to rid me. The fellow cannot take a hint, and is the most intolerable annoyance to me."

" A cousin of Lady Bohun's?"

" Yes; on leave of absence from his regiment. I believe his colonel has forgotten his existence, for the leave seems interminable. He makes this house his home in the coolest way I ever saw, and has at this moment possession of the room that ought to be yours."

Two other couples had fallen into *sotto voce* conversations in other parts of the room; Mrs.

Blackstone and Mrs. Washington sitting so close together that the artificial flowers in their respective caps touched, and Lady Bohun and Captain Aylmer pretending to play at draughts, this being the only game the fair Euphemia professed, and certainly one eminently suited to the abilities and capacity of her companion.

"So that is Mr. Bohun," said Mrs. Washington. "I recollect him now. He sat by me at Phemy's wedding. My dear friend, I had no idea he lived in the house."

"In what house?" asked Mrs. Blackstone, whose hearing was very imperfect.

"Bohun Court, my dear. I found out at dinner that that is his regular home. How does Phemy like that?"

"Oh! delighted."

"That's very amiable of her. I don't think it is a good plan, and Mr. B. looks to me like a man of great determination. If I were Phemy, I would not continue it, particularly in Sir Felix's state."

"Oh! he has nothing whatever to do with the estate. He had at first, but Phemy has gradually taken it out of his hands."

"And very right of her, too; not that that was what I said; but it doesn't signify. What I meant was, that there being no heir, and in Sir Felix's state of health—you understand me, my dear—a brother of that firm temper (for I can see it in his mouth and chin) may get rather too large a slice, eh?"

"A slice of what?" asked Mrs. Blackstone, getting sleepy.

"Loaves and fishes, my dear."

"No fishing at all, I believe, but I'll ask Phemy. I have never been down there yet, but we accompany her on her return, I think."

"I'm glad to hear it. A young thing like that wants a mother's eye to look after her interests, &c.......you understand me, my dear......and there is another point I wanted to talk over with you—that maid of hers......"

"That Bohun Court may be hers?" said Mrs. Blackstone trying hard to keep awake and answer coherently. "Oh! there is not the slightest shadow of a doubt as to Bohun Court being Phemy's, at all events for her life, if anything happens to Sir Felix, poor dear man!"

"That is not what I said. I spoke of that maid of hers, Ponsford, who seems to me to have gained a very undue influence over Phemy. Phemy spoils her, and the woman is gaining a dangerous ascendancy. Don't you see it?"

"See what? No, I see nothing particular; I beg pardon, my dear friend, but Sydney does laugh so loud......what was there to see? Are they not playing at draughts?"

"I'm talking of Ponsford," persisted Mrs. Washington, in an offended whisper, "Phemy's maid—but you are going to sleep, my dear."

"Indeed, I am not," retorted Mrs. Blackstone, angrily; "I was merely closing my eyes. What of Ponsford?"

But at this moment Mrs. Washington saw that her conversation had attracted the attention of both Phemy and Mr. Bohun, so she wisely discontinued it, and went and sat down by Sir Felix.

"Phemy," whispered Captain Aylmer, as he pondered gravely over the moves of his game, "I would do a good deal to oblige you, but don't set me down again to play third person after dinner with Sir Felix and his brother. Mr. Bohun looked ready to eat me all the time I was left unprotected there by you in charge of your husband; and as for Sir Felix, never did man breathe such broad hints to get me out of the room, yet I remained firm to my post."

"Good boy. To-morrow I will ask somebody

else to relieve you; but till I do, I cannot let you off."

" You don't like Mr.......eh?"

" Can't *endure*......"

" Skeleton in the cupboard, eh?"

" Hush!......don't let Mrs. Washington hear that, or else......"

" Phemy, my dear," exclaimed Sir Felix, suddenly, " Guy's going. Have we any engagements for to-morrow?"

" It depends on how you are, dear Sir Felix."

" Then, Guy, come early, and we can settle our plans when the morrow arrives."

And thus closed the first evening.

CHAPTER XX.

DAY after day passed, till the days numbered a
week, and the system displayed on the first
evening of Mr. Bohun's arrival in town, was so
strictly followed up, that on looking back, he
found to his surprise that, without being in the
least able to account for it, he had been entirely
unable during the whole of that time to have a
single hour's private conversation with his brother,
or indeed ever to find himself alone with him for
more than five minutes.

Yet this did not seem done on purpose. He
could not declare that it was intentional. If it
were so, it was so cleverly arranged that it left
him no power to complain, inasmuch as he could
never decidedly say he was denied an audience in
private.

He went to the house early. Lady Bohun,
like an exemplary wife, would be reading the

newspaper to her husband. He waited patiently till that was over, and her ladyship would say, "There, now I shall leave you for a gossip." Before he had time to enter fully upon the interest of any subject, Ponsford would glide in.

"If you please, Sir Felix, would it be convenient for me to rub your feet now? This is just a moment that her ladyship can spare me."

The rubbing was a great interruption, and sometimes appeared a vexatious one to the invalid; but still it certainly was a great relief to him, so it was submitted to, and Mr. Bohun had to draw in again. Sir Felix spoke very openly before Ponsford. He went running on, on matters of business, in a manner which surprised his brother; but Mr. Bohun could not bring himself to do this, consequently, all this was lost time to him, and he would make up his mind to wait till her hour of attendance had expired.

No sooner did she leave the room, and he thought to be quiet, than the door re-opened.

"Luncheon, Sir Felix," and in tripped Lady Bohun, to give her husband a dutiful arm; saying, as she did so, "What a pleasure to you, dear Sir Felix, to have such a nice companion all the morning. How good of Mr. Bohun, for he tells me he came up to town on business. We must not take up all his time though, must we?"

At luncheon, friends, or father, or mother, or cousin, would be sure to drop in, and extend the meal to the length of a dinner party. Then Sir Felix would go exhausted to his own room, and Lady Bohun would whisper to her brother-in-law,

"Let him rest—sometimes he dozes—he is ordered not to talk after his meals. Would you like to sit with him, or shall I? I generally work by his side without opening my lips. Would you like a book?"

Yes. Mr. Bohun would take a book, and sure enough Sir Felix *would* go to sleep, and then came the door again.

"Carriage at the door, Sir Felix. My lady quite ready," she having taken about ten minutes only to adorn herself.

Then Mr. Bohun would go out driving with them. Lady Bohun by his side, Mrs. Blackstone and Sir Felix opposite to them; and they would take a long drive up to Hampstead, or round by Willesden, and Sir Felix would come home in another state of exhaustion; and then, as they helped him out of the carriage, he would say, "I am not strong, Guy," and Lady Bohun, with a pretty air of sadness, would say, "You see how weak he is, but don't be alarmed, he will rally by dinner time."

At dinner, people joined the table every day—either one or two strangers, gentlemen, being invariably invited, "just to break the family party," Lady Bohun would say. And then the evening ended as the first had done. Day after day, always the same. Sir Felix was never alone, and yet how could Mr. Bohun complain?—he could not. What had he to complain of?—nothing tangible. Could he boldly desire a private conversation with his brother—no, not with a devoted wife who took every opportunity of insinuating that she and Sir Felix had but one thought, and one heart, and one mind.

Yet all he wished to say was very little. Why did he make such a mountain of his molehill? It was merely to inform his brother that he had resolved that henceforth their homes should be separate; yet he shrank from communicating this information in presence of a third person. Why? —because of the opposition the determination might meet? No!—but because he dreaded the ready acquiescence! He dreaded the sparkle of Lady Bohun's eye, and the insincerity of her silvery-toned regrets. He dreaded the facilities

she would place in furtherance of his plans, and
the insurmountable, yet almost imperceptible,
obstacles she would raise, should Sir Felix, for
once in a way, rouse up like an outraged lion, and
implore his brother still to remain under the
roof which had sheltered both equally from
childhood.

The anger or the sorrow of Sir Felix would be
easier to bear than the ill-concealed triumph of
Lady Bohun. Yet, mortifying as it would be, he
must go through it. He must hear the regrets,
and pretend to believe them; he must see the
triumph, and pretend to be blind !

"Mrs. Trant was right," thought he to himself
one day; "she has shaken me off, and yet it has
been without a struggle. I came to town prepared to think the point would be contested, yet
she has succeeded in her aim and end without a
word, and without descending from her pedestal.
Lady Bohun, you have paved the way so well,
that I see I shall be permitted to resign my post
without opposition. So be it."

And forthwith Mr. Bohun set about the business
that had brought him up to town—the arrangement of the *pied-à-terre* which he was in future
to rejoice in as his own.

In the course of this transaction, chance threw

him in the way of one of the partners in the firm of Bland and Frumpton, his family solicitors. It was Mr. Bland who happened to be in the office when Mr. Bohun, passing the door, looked in to say how do you do.

Mr. Bland, gay and *debonnaire*, was always charmed to see visitors, whether clients or friends; whilst Mr. Frumpton, over head and ears in parchments, played the working bee in the most praiseworthy manner, and never uttered an unnecessary word—yet one partner had just as much to do as the other, in point of fact, but they had different ways of doing it.

Mr. Bland's delight at the apparition of one of the brothers of Bohun Court was very vociferous, and he nailed him to a chair instantly. It was so long since he had seen him, he really must detain him for a few minutes, and he kept Mr. Bohun in close conversation for two hours.

Yet the subject was sufficiently interesting to render the detention far from irksome. They talked entirely about Sir Felix, and Mr. Bohun gleaned an immense amount of information.

"When your brother first came to town, my dear sir," said Mr. Bland, in the course of his ramblings, "we saw a good deal of him—sometimes he came here, sometimes we went there—

N 2

but lately, somehow, we have not been so much in his confidence. We are aware that we are not his only counsellors; we do not presume to question his perfect right to select his own advisers, but, at the same time, my dear sir, we are quite aware that he has sought legal assistance in other quarters. Of course, these things are well known amongst us—it is no affair of ours, but we know all the same. And, indeed, I expected it some time ago—ever since Sir Felix withdrew some of his papers from our charge."

Mr. Bohun was going to speak, but changed his mind and sat silent, so Mr. Bland proceeded.

"Of course, we always imagined and anticipated that from time to time Sir Felix would find it incumbent on him to make alterations in his testamentary documents, and we felt somewhat hurt at the moment that we were not to be honoured with his confidence; however, as we were saying ......but, my dear sir, you look very pale—let us offer you a glass of wine?"

An unpleasant idea had flashed on Mr. Bohun all at once, at this accidental disclosure; and, much to his vexation, he had actually felt himself turn pale; yet why? He had suddenly awoke to the fact that Sir Felix had no doubt been making a new will, yet what was that to him?

Nothing—and he would have felt it as nothing had there been no mystery about it; but if, indeed it were nothing to him, why all this concealment and mystery? Why had the will been withdrawn from the hands of Messrs. Bland and Frumpton? Why had strange lawyers (for now he recollected what the old butler had said about the "strange gentlemen" who had "worretted and fidgetted" Sir Felix) been called in, and such secrecy been observed? So Mr. Bohun turned pale, but he was angry with himself for doing so; angry to think that he could for one instant suspect his brother of any act which could by any possibility come under the designation of treachery, much less injury, to himself.

But still, Bohun Court was not entailed. It was in the power of Sir Felix to leave it to any mortal being he pleased. Since his marriage, little conversation had passed between the brothers, but even that little had served to set the mind of Mr. Bohun at rest as to the ultimate destination of the well-beloved home of his childhood. Sir Felix had distinctly given him to understand that, failing an heir (or an heiress), Bohun Court would revert to him. Once indeed, he uttered some very decided words about it. They were these: "I once thought how bit-

terly vexed and disappointed I should be if the
wife of my choice did not see Bohun Court with
our eyes; but now, Guy, I am actually not
sorry. That Euphemia has not given her heart
to the old place makes my way clear before me."

There was surely no mistaking these words;
at least, so Mr. Bohun thought, *till now;* but now
he by no means felt so sure of his ground. It
seemed pretty evident that the will had been
withdrawn for a purpose; that Lady Bohun was
aware of the withdrawal; and that *he* was to be
kept in ignorance of it, and this augured ill.

" What can she have been plotting and planning?" thought he, as Mr. Bland rattled glasses in
a deep cupboard under one of his windows.
"How can one so green in age, have learned to
be so gray in artifice?"

" By the by," exclaimed Mr. Bland, at last
emerging with a little round tray, on which was
a bottle of curaçoa; " what a very singular coincidence it is, that that extraordinary young person who was confidential servant in the family of
old Lady Merivale for so many years, should have
found her way back to Bohun Court again."

" Ponsford?" said Mr. Bohun, absently; " yes,
but why is she extraordinary?"

" Singular woman—a *most* singular woman !"

proceeded the old lawyer, pinching in his lips; " there is no female of all our acquaintance that has given us more trouble and perplexity than that Mrs. Ponsford, so singularly has she been mixed up in the affairs of many of our clients."

" Ah! you mean Lady Mary Topham and the jewel case ?"

" That is one instance. Goodness me! the trouble we had with the family about those pearls! Mr. Topham swore Lady Mary never could have given them, but Mrs. Ponsford had her documents all safe and correct. No want of black and white, and then to our infinite embarrassment, Mr. Topham declared the black and white was very unlike his wife's usual handwriting! Bless my heart, what a breeze we had here, but there has been a worse than that since. That blew over, for what could we say against black and white? The pearls were left to the individual, and she made us a low curtsey and carried them off in triumph, and we thought we had said good-bye to her, but not she! she turned up a little while ago, on the death of Lady Merivale."

" That was a very awkward story," said Mr. Bohun, " all the world knows it; did not the wife of the second son see, through the half-open door,

Ponsford holding the old lady's fingers round the pen that signed that most nefarious codicil?"

" By which the old lady left all her plate to that young doctor of her's? Yes—(to whom I verily believe Mrs. Ponsford was at the time engaged), though he wisely turned it into money soon after he came into possession, and still more wisely did *not* marry Mrs. Ponsford. But however......what we meant by calling her extraordinary was this, that she has the faculty of obtaining over those with whom she resides, and who are worth her trouble, the most marvellous influence, we would almost venture to say, the most dangerous influence."

" You are right," said Mr. Bohun, emphatically, " I have seen it."

" So have I," returned Mr. Bland, shortly.

" Any case in point?" asked Mr. Bohun.

" Yes, she turns Lady Bohun round her finger already," answered the old man, courageously.

" I am sorry to hear it," was Mr. Bohun's grave reply.

" And, my dear sir, if that were the extent of her power we should not presume to complain— complain is hardly the word—we mean, presume to offer a word of warning, but we fear the evil will not rest here. The last time we had the honour of waiting on Sir Felix was on the occasion of the transfer of......bless me, what was it?"

Mr. Bland was a great talker; great talkers sometimes get themselves into a tangle, and are on the verge of telling secrets, and when this happened to Mr. Bland, he was sharp enough to pretend to lose the thread of his discourse, or forget the point of his story.

"I know to what you refer," said Mr. Bohun, calmly; "but what has that got to do with Mrs. Ponsford?"

"My dear sir, it was on that occasion that we saw, with regret and dread, the growing influence she was gaining over your brother. Had we not known her previous history and all about her, we might have thought nothing of it, but as it was, we certainly did think to ourselves, to use a homely phrase, the lady is at her old tricks again, for not a sentence did Sir Felix utter, but what he added, turning to her, 'Isn't that what I said I would do, Ponsford?' Oh! Mr. Bohun, my dear sir," exclaimed Mr. Bland, suddenly springing up in a startling manner, "that's a dangerous woman. Believe me, it may some day be necessary for you to be on your guard, and we take the liberty of old friendship to tell you so."

Mr. Bohun did not spend the rest of that day comfortably. Although he had a good deal of business to transact, still, as he walked hurriedly from place to place, he had time enough to think, and his thoughts were disagreeable ones.

Doubt and distrust had entered into his mind, and though it seemed like ingratitude and injustice towards his brother to doubt him, still he could not help having fears that Sir Felix, no longer his own agent, had been worked on, during his stay in town, by influences far more powerful than his own enfeebled will, and if so, what might he not have done?

For money, Mr. Bohun cared nothing. He had enough and more of his own than he wanted, but for Bohun Court—he worshipped every tuft of moss on those ivy-covered walls! Surely, surely, it would never pass away from him?

And then wild thoughts flitted through his brain, making the sober man half delirious—she would be a gay widow, were she to become one—she was very young, and might long outlive him—he might offer to purchase the beloved place of her, and she might refuse!—and then he pulled his hat over his eyes, and hurried on, he hardly knew which way, and looked back with a groan in his heart, on the day when Sir Felix, in a weak hour, had for the third time, placed his liberty in another's keeping.

But Guy Bohun was too high-minded to indulge long in thoughts like these : they had tortured him for the time, but that once over, he was himself again; the memory of all that he heard that day clung to him, but the bitterness of it passed, and a quiet evening spent by himself, brought back sufficient tranquillity to his spirit to enable him to present himself the next morning at his brother's house without a single feeling of animosity or reproach.

What he heard, however, when he went in, surprised him.

CHAPTER XXI.

ALL going to Bohun Court? The whole family
on the move, when, four-and-twenty hours pre-
viously, no such intention had been even breathed?

"Yes, sir. Sir Felix gave the order last night,
sir, and Mr. Burley went down this morning."

It was one of the new footmen who spoke, and
when Mr. Bohun heard that it was Burley who
had been selected as the *avant-courier*, he at once
saw that there was not the slightest chance of his
discovering the real reason of the sudden flight.
Though not naturally suspicious, he was becoming so by degrees, and his present suspicion was,
that the old butler had not been sent out of the
way without a motive. The frequent *têtes-à-tête*
which the ancient domestic managed to steal, had
evidently been observed and disapproved, so, in
order that no truths should be told, he was sent
out of the way of being asked questions.

Mr. Bohun entered the house in silence, perhaps rather a morose silence, and was roused by
the voice whose unvarying cheerfulness had become quite a source of irritation to him—Mr.
Aylmer's.

"How d'ye do, Mr. Bohun? Ain't we in a
confusion? I'm going to have a cigar to purify
the house."

"Lady Bohun is very forbearing if she permits
you such an indulgence," returned Mr. Bohun,
well remembering how early in her married career
it was denied to *him*.

"Oh! Phemy don't mind. If she did, I don't
care; I'm privileged. Are you going in to see
the old gen......I beg your pardon......I mean Sir
Felix?"

Mr. Bohun said nothing; but passed on towards his brother's room. Sydney Aylmer put
his head into the dining-room, the lighted cigar
between his fingers.

"Phemy, old Growler's gone into Sir Felix's
room. He looks like thunder."

"Thank you, Sydney; go and talk till I can
come."

"Impossible, Phemy......I've just lighted my
pipe of consolation."

" Oh ! you odious creature ! then I suppose I *must......*"

And she swept all the papers by which she was surrounded into her writing-table drawer. This took her several minutes, during which time Mr. Bohun sat by his brother's chair, Sir Felix looking nervously up into his face, having greeted him still more so.

" My dear Guy......alone for a moment at last! and such volumes to say," he began, in a sort of gasping way; "we are off, as you see......I could bear it no longer......that fellow Aylmer and all these confounded friends and relations......I am worn to death, and said so, and somehow, before I knew where I was, Euphemia had settled it all, and thought it best for me to go and be quiet a little......otherwise, my dear Guy, this is the very last moment I should have chosen to leave town ......just during your stay......and I wanted so much to speak to you......but follow as soon as you can......it is important......there's somebody at the door .....just look."

" Does Sir Felix mind my cigar?" said a voice.

" No !—devil take his cigar and him, too. No, Mr. Aylmer, not if the door is shut. There, Guy, bang the door, never mind politeness with that insufferably cool coxcomb. Now, to business

......abruptly, or we shall be sure to be interrupted."

"Be calm, Felix," said the more temperate brother, "there is no hurry."

"Yes, but there *is*," whispered Sir Felix, "much more than you think. I have something to explain to you that *must* be explained, lest you should misjudge."

"My dear Felix," interrupted Mr. Bohun, taking his brother's trembling hands within his own, "I should never do that : make your mind perfectly easy that I should never misjudge you under *any* circumstances."

"Not *me*, Guy, not misjudge *me*—I did not mean that, but misjudge those whose future happiness and comfort I have naturally very much at heart......"

"Naturally—yes—well?"

"And you must not think, my dear Guy, nor must Bland and Frumpton think, because I have not consulted them in this instance, that I have no longer the highest opinion of their talents ..... and......and......"

"Felix," said Mr. Bohun, gravely, "you are not accountable to any human being for your actions, and with whatever you do, I have no doubt I shall......I mean......"

It was now Mr. Bohun who stammered. He had taken his seat by Sir Felix, so strongly possessed with the idea that he was about to have the secret of alterations in the will imparted to him, that he was actually on the point of forgiving his brother for what had never been divulged!

But Sir Felix had worked himself up into such a pitch of nervous agitation, that he seemed to take no notice of any part of his brother's sentence except the words, " you are not accountable to any human being," and to these only he replied.

" True—exactly—just what I wished to explain, that I abhor tyranny, influence, and all that sort of thing; I am my own master. Certainly, I would rather have remained in town just now, but, you see, I am very far from well. Ponsford begins to understand my constitution......"

Mr. Bohun drew in a deep breath.

" Oh !" continued Sir Felix, misunderstanding its import, " there really is nothing serious the matter with me, only constant change of air and scene seems requisite, and though your visit up to town happens most unfortunately, still......"

The door opened, and Lady Bohun, radiant, as usual, looked in.

" Ah ! Mr. Bohun ! Dear Sir Felix, I want

Mr. Bohun here a moment, just to give an opinion on my alabaster group......"

She took him into the hall, "......a little pious fraud of mine, Mr. Bohun; but I want to tell you of our sudden departure. We are always obliged to take Sir Felix when the spirit moves him; if we did not, we could do nothing, he is so painfully nervous. Therefore, if you please, not a word to deter him; he is quite charmed at the idea of seeing Bohun Court again, and so am I " (" news," thought Mr. Bohun); "but now I must go back to him; come in, and we hope, dear Sir Felix, don't we? that your brother will follow us as soon as ever it is agreeable to him."

Thanks for the permission, again thought Mr. Bohun. But she was at her post again, and the interview was over; the opportunity had come, and was gone; and now she sat, holding the hand of Sir Felix, and looking earnestly in his face. A dew of perspiration certainly did stand on his forehead.

" You have been agitating yourself," said she; " you look quite upset, dear Sir Felix. You must have a glass of port wine instantly. No?—then it must be your tonic—yes, your tonic, dearest Sir Felix, if you love me! there's a dear good patient! Please, Mr. Bohun, ring the bell—

twice—many thanks. Twice means for Ponsford;
she knows our quantity."

The opportunity was over indeed, and what
could Mr. Bohun do? What had he done? What
was he doing? Sitting there like a mummy, seeing his brother treated like a child, and powerless
to act, for was this a moment to announce to that
trembling man a piece of intelligence which, even
in his days of health, he always met with almost
angry opposition?

"I must write it," thought Mr. Bohun, and
thus he resigned himself to the circumstances of
the moment.

And how had it all been arranged! To explain
it, we must go back a day.

The morning spent by Mr. Bohun in the office
of Messrs. Bland and Frumpton, was one destined
by Euphemia to be passed at the Crystal Palace.
She had made up a party, consisting of all her
most agreeable intimates, and had arranged that
they should all dine there, Sir Felix should be
wheeled about in a Bath chair (which he detested), that she should enjoy her usual noisy
flirtation with Mr. Aylmer, and that in the cool
of the evening all should drive home to a late
supper, Sir Felix being consigned to his bed
before that part of the entertainment commenced.

Mr. Bohun had been invited, but not in terms which he would have condescended to accept, even had he wished to join the party, which he did not.

"I suppose you would not care to make one of our number?" had been Lady Bohun's words; "I am not the least superstitious about thirteen at table, if you would like to join us?"

"I thank you," Mr. Bohun had replied, "but I have quite an accumulation of business on hand for that day, so you need not brave the unlucky number on *my* account."

It so happened that when the morning dawned, Ponsford asked leave to absent herself from her duties for a few hours, as soon as she had arrayed her mistress in her morning toilette. She was obliged to see a lawyer who paid her a small annuity, left as a legacy to her; she would be sure to be back by two o'clock, in time to dress her ladyship for the Crystal Palace, if she might be permitted to start early. So at ten o'clock Mrs. Ponsford, delicately attired in silver gray, with the prettiest of simple straw bonnets, and a little veil, covered with black spots, tied close over her face (making her look like a patched beauty of many reigns ago), set forth on her errand.

But instead of an absence of three hours, which Lady Bohun expected, back came the damsel in less than one.

" Why, Ponsford," exclaimed her mistress, "your business did not take long."

"Oh! my lady, I was not able to transact it."

" No?—what a pity, after having all the trouble of going to the ends of the earth and making such a *belle toilette.*"

" Oh, my lady !"—with that passive, resigned smile of hers—"the trouble was very little, only it was vexatious. However, as it happened to be Mr. Bohun......"

Euphemia rather drew up. " Mr. Bohun what?" said she.

" Mr. Bohun was already with Mr. Bland when I arrived......I hope, my lady, I am not committing an indiscretion......of course I was not supposed to know he was there; and, of course, if he had wished his visit known, he would have mentioned it. But, perhaps, your ladyship *did* know......?"

" Not I. What could he be there about, Ponsford?"

" I have not an idea—at least, I cannot say, my lady—business, of course."

" What business, I wonder? Nothing connected with *us*, I am sure; for I have taken good care, and so have you, have you not? that he should not worry Sir Felix on business matters. Now what *could* he be doing at Bland's?"

Conscience may well be said to make cowards of us all. The hearts of both those fair confederates misgave them because of the simple fact of Mr. Bohun's being found in a lawyer's office.

" I met Mr. Frumpton on the stairs, my lady, and he said Mr. Bland was engaged. I said I had but little time and few opportunities; but when he mentioned that it was Mr. Bohun, and that he had already been there more than an hour, I thought I had better come home again, and just name it to your ladyship."

" How lucky ! I am so glad you found it out, Ponsford; but it is very unfortunate his having gone there—very unfortunate—most provoking! and after all our pains, too, and all my anxiety."

" Mr. Bohun can do no harm, my lady," said Ponsford, in a very low voice.

" How do we know ?" replied Euphemia, in the same tone.

" The new will is signed and witnessed, my lady."

" But Sir Felix may make fifty codicils ?"

" Not without your knowledge, my lady, unless Mr. Bohun should have sufficient influence or opportunity to induce him to do so."

" He has influence with Sir Felix to make him do anything!" exclaimed Lady Bohun vehemently. (She did not see Ponsford's smile again, though generally it was a book to her—a book full of hints and suspicions.) " He might do incalculable mischief even now! How do I know but what he has drawn everything out of that old chatterbox, Burley, and formed his resolutions accordingly? Ponsford, we are in a difficulty!"

" Not the least, my lady, indeed!"

" No? I think we *are*, though, and I should be very glad if you could prove the contrary."

" My lady, no harm can be done, even now, provided Sir Felix and Mr. Bohun are prevented being alone together."

" But what a task it is to prevent that! I am sure I am sometimes at my wit's end, and Mr. Aylmer often declares he will not be continually mounting guard. As for me, I am tired out, and I dare say you are, too."

" Oh, my lady, I would do anything to serve you! Perhaps I ought not to say so, but it would have gone to my heart to have seen your ladyship left, as it were, at Mr. Bohun's mercy, if anything happened to Sir Felix."

" But, Ponsford, I don't feel safe even now! what *can* we do? If Mr. Bohun sees the new

will, he will oppose it—he will terrify Sir Felix—
Sir Felix will give way, and then......Oh, Pons-
ford ! what *could* take that man to Bland and
Frumpton's ?"

" My lady, do not agitate yourself. I think we
can avert any mischief. I mean, I think your
ladyship can win the game yet."

" Oh, Ponsford ! I would give anybody fifty
pounds if they could just get Mr. Bohun out
of the way till we go back to Bohun Court
again."

Ponsford's smile returned.

" Ponsford, you have some scheme. What is
it ?   An anonymous letter, saying Hector is
poisoned ?"

" My lady, I would undertake to prevent Mr.
Bohun's having any private conversation with Sir
Felix for much less than fifty pounds."

" Ponsford, you are a jewel, if you are in earnest.
Is it a feasible plan ?   I declare I would give
twenty pounds."

" It is quite a feasible plan if you take it in
hand yourself, my lady."

" That I will, with all my heart !   Ponsford,
what shall I give you ?   Choose—quick—not
twenty pounds, though, I was joking !   Not
money—you don't care for money !   Now, I tell

you what—you shall have my black moiré antique, if you do it !"

" Oh, thank you, my lady ! but it is your lady-ship, not I."

" Well, but what is it?"

" Sir Felix was very anxious to go to Bohun Court the other day, my lady, just before Mr. Bohun came—after Mr. Melville was in town."

" I remember, so he was; well ?"

" If he were to go now, my lady ?"

" And leave Mr. Bohun in town ?   Very good. But suppose he were instantly to follow us ?"

" He will not yet, my lady ; if at all."

" Ponsford ?"

" Perhaps I am betraying a confidence; but from you, my lady, somehow I feel as if I could conceal nothing.   Mr. Bohun has taken, or has almost taken, some chambers at the Albany, kept by a relation of mine."

Euphemia clasped her hands in- speechless delight.

" He would not be likely to leave town at this moment, therefore, my lady, and if you could persuade Sir Felix to start directly......"

" It shall be done, Ponsford—we could go to-morrow even, if you could go down by this evening's train."

"Would it not be better to send Mr. Burley, my lady? to get *him* out of the way, my lady?"

"Burley? I don't know how we could spare him. Sir Felix might not like it."

"If Mr. Burley is here when Mr. Bohun calls again......" insinuated Ponsford.

"I see, I see," cried Euphemia, "you are quite right; it shall be Burley, and I will settle it all with Sir Felix myself."

So Lady Bohun dressed for the Crystal Palace, expatiated on the beauties of nature during the whole drive to Sydenham, spoke to Sir Felix incessantly of the loveliness of Bohun Court in summer—wished she were there at that moment to see it; and ended, by having it all her own way.

END OF VOL. I.

O